FROM A HIGH THIN WIRE

Other Fiction by Joan Clark

Swimming Toward the Light

The Victory of Geraldine Gull

Eriksdottir

Latitudes of Melt

FROM A

HIGH

THIN

WIRE

JOAN CLARK

First published by NeWest Press, 1982. This trade edition published by Goose Lane Editions, 2004.

Cover illustration by Veer Incorporated.
Cover and interior design by Paul Vienneau.
Printed in Canada by Transcontinental.
10 9 8 7 6 5 4 3 2 1

National Library of Canada Cataloguing in Publication Data

Clark, Joan, 1934-
    From a high thin wire / Joan Clark. — 2nd ed.

ISBN 0-86492-385-6

    I. Title.

PS8555.L37F7 2004   C813'.54   C2004-900619-3

Published with the financial support of the Canada Council for the Arts, the Government of Canada through the Book Publishing Industry Development Program, and the New Brunswick Culture and Sports Secretariat.

Goose Lane Editions
469 King Street
Fredericton, New Brunswick
CANADA E3B 1E5

www.gooselane.com

For Mary Gail MacDonald

Contents

God's Country

From the beginning, Emily felt self-conscious about taking the mine tour. Anybody would feel slightly foolish taking a tour in her old hometown, paying money, buying a ticket to view something she'd grown up with. It was a bald admission of ignorance, of not having known enough about Sydney Mines when she'd lived here, of having missed something so important that after another life somewhere else, in Emily's case twenty years, she had to come back to find it.

Though she had disguised herself as a social studies teacher who was here to learn something about the mining industry, Emily knew she was fooling herself. She couldn't help wanting the man in the ticket booth to have the angular face and brown eyes of Damien Roscoe. But the man in front of her pushing a ticket through the makeshift window was short and blue-eyed. She was annoyed at herself for expecting to see Damien. It would be pure coincidence to find him here; and anyway, what did she think they could possibly say to each other after all these years?

Emily went outside and sat on a bench in the sun. The bench was lobster red and shiny, as if it had been painted the day before. She leaned back against the grey shed and closed her eyes, remembering how, when she lived here, the daughter of schoolteacher parents, she had thought of miners as going off to war, knowing that those men who left their houses every morning tunnelled underneath the ocean in a black trench roofed over by sea bottom. A no man's land. People seldom spoke of it, of the casualties: the cave-ins, the gassings, the accidents. No one would have toured the pit any more than they would have toured a minefield. Back then it wasn't customary for buses of schoolchildren to be driven to factories, plants and mines for social studies projects. It was enough to see the miners downtown Saturday night before the nine o'clock show, spending their wages in the British-Canadian Co-op, the People's Store, the OK. It was enough to see them reeling out of the tavern onto the cinder parking lot, cursing and brawling. And then in church Sunday mornings, faces scrubbed red and cowlicks plastered down, sitting there subdued, good Christian soldiers.

"Be another ten minutes yet." A dapper man wearing a bow tie and white shirt beneath overalls had come out of the shed and was walking toward Emily. He stuck out his hand. "Jim Macdonald's the name."

Emily gave him her name. "But I used to be a Prentice," she said.

Mr. Macdonald tipped back his hard hat and scratched his head. "Prentice. Prentice. Don't I know that name from somewheres?"

"My parents were teachers here. I grew up in Sydney Mines."

"So that's it. I knew the name was familiar." Then, pretending to scold, Mr. Macdonald said, "What's the matter with you that you're not living here now?"

"I live out West with my family. I teach school there."

"One of those blue-eyed Arabs, eh?" He shot her a sly look. "Getting rich off us poor fellas down here."

Emily didn't rise to the bait. Mr. Macdonald knew as well as she did that Cape Breton oil came from Venezuela, not Alberta.

From a High Thin Wire

"You don't need oil," she said, challenging him. "Look at the coal." She nodded toward the black mounds near the railway tracks; the heaps, they were called. "You can burn those."

"Nobody wants our coal," Mr. Macdonald said. "That's why the colliery shut down."

"Well, at least there's enough to keep the furnaces here going for a long time," Emily said.

Mr. Macdonald laughed at that. "You been gone a long time, lady," he said. "Our coal furnaces were hauled away to the scrap pile years ago and replaced by oil furnaces. A crying shame it was, but we can't turn back the clock, now can we?"

Emily studied the faces of the three miners who sat opposite her. None of them looked familiar. She wasn't sure she'd recognize Damien Roscoe even if she did see him. She had a newspaper photograph of him back home in her photo album, but it was fuzzy grey, out-of-focus; it wasn't any more use than the photograph which hung in an oval frame on her bedroom wall in Calgary. The photograph was of her dead grandmother, whom she'd never seen.

The Roscoes had lived in the house next door. They had come from Wales, where Mr. Roscoe's father and grandfather had been miners. Mr. Roscoe was tall, black-haired and fierce. His skin was so dark that Emily used to imagine that coal dust had gotten into his pores and into his blood, that his spit was black, even the wax in his ears. She was always surprised when he appeared on his porch or in the parlour window without his shirt, his long underwear unbuttoned to the waist, showing an incongruously pale chest, the hairs like black wires stuck into a peeled potato. Sometimes when he was dressed like this, he would sing hymns. He sang tenor, standing beside the piano in the parlour while Peggy, the eldest, played. Danny and Damien sang too, and Megan, the youngest. Even timid Mrs. Roscoe.

Mr. Roscoe had gotten a choir together, miners who enjoyed

singing. They never sang publicly. They never got that far. It was Mr. Roscoe's temper that broke them up. It was nothing for him to jab someone in the chest if he didn't like what was said, to fling a plate across the room if the food didn't suit. Both Danny and Damien had been bruised by his belt. Sometimes Mr. Roscoe roared so loud it seemed the shingles of his house shuddered. Emily was always on guard against these dark and sudden outbursts. Even when he was sitting placidly on his front step in his underwear, Emily knew that Mr. Roscoe had only momentarily stepped out of his bearskin, that it was hanging on the hook in the hallway ready to be put back on. Sometimes if she was sitting on the veranda, he would call out pleasantries to her about the freshness of the breeze, the greenness of the grass and how she was doing in school.

Emily never allowed herself to be drawn past a polite response. She thought being friendly toward Mr. Roscoe somehow betrayed Damien's confidence in her. It was Damien who had told her about the beatings and the smashed china.

Damien looked like his father's paper cut-out. He was tall and thin, with black hair and fair skin, but he had none of his father's robustness. Those times when he was in bed with bronchitis, Emily brought him his homework, and throughout junior high school they did their homework together: colouring maps, writing definitions out of the same dictionary, copying each other's notes.

Whenever Emily brought home Damien's work, Mrs. Roscoe ushered her into the parlour. By then, Damien was downstairs waiting for her, sitting on the chesterfield in his blue-checkered bathrobe. Emily kept her eyes off the hair that was beginning to show on his legs where his pyjamas rode up. She didn't want any reminders that Damien was becoming a man, that he would one day need the same things of her she thought her father needed. She avoided looking at the whisker eruptions on his chin, the tapered strength of his fingers. Instead she concentrated on the cleanliness and order of the Roscoe's parlour. Because it was so different from her mother's careless housekeeping. Every spring Mrs. Roscoe repapered walls, painted woodwork, washed doilies and polished the piano, with its shrine of family photos on top. After Emily had showed Damien his assignments, Mrs. Roscoe came in with tea and cookies on a tray. The teacups were Dutch blue with houses on them. Emily never got used to this. She felt like royalty. As if something more than delivering homework was expected of her. At home, her parents served tea in mugs. Visitors had to shove books off chairs in order to sit down. Emily interpreted the good china as meaning Mrs. Roscoe approved of her as Damien's girlfriend. She was uncomfortable with this possibility. In her mind's eye, the word *girlfriend* loomed large on a billboard with DANGER and WARNING stickers pasted on top.

Damien was the only Roscoe who was good at school. Peggy had quit grade nine to work as a housekeeper at the hospital. It was too soon to tell about Megan; she was only in grade one. Danny hated school. He wanted to quit, Damien said, but the old man wouldn't let him. He was determined to send Danny to a conservatory for voice lessons, something he had always wanted to do himself. Danny wanted to work in the pit and went there every chance he got. Damien couldn't figure out why anyone would choose to work in such a dark, stinking hole. He'd gone down once with the old man and that was enough. It was so bloody cold he couldn't keep his teeth from chattering. He wanted to get as far away from Sydney Mines as he could. Whenever he talked to Emily about his future, Damien always spoke with fearless bravado; there was nothing he couldn't do. After graduation he was getting a job in the city, but only for a year or two until he earned the money for voice lessons. Then he'd get a scholarship to university and work toward a music degree. Someday he'd be a famous singer. He was fifteen when he told Emily this.

"Whatever happened to the Roscoe boys?" Emily said, though she already knew about Danny. Mr. Macdonald and she had been going over different people in town, seeing whom they had both known, so it was inevitable that they should come to the Roscoes.

"Danny's on TV. You must've seen him," Mr. Macdonald said. "Or don't you bother watching us down here in God's country? Maybe" — he gave her a sidelong look — "maybe you watch all them Yankee programs."

On Saturday nights, Emily liked to go downstairs to watch Jolly Danny Roscoe on TV, which she preferred doing alone. She never lost the wonder of someone from back home being on her television screen, a wonder she could never explain to her husband and kids. Danny was one of the stars on the *Cape Breton Islanders Show*; the other star was hymn singer Gracie Murphy. Danny moved across the floor in the graceful shuffle Emily had come to expect of fat people. He'd taken up tap dancing, she'd supposed, because his voice had run out from hard living and drink. Sometimes he'd take a mouth organ out of his pocket and puff good-naturedly into it, but he could only play with one hand, so it wasn't done with any skill; it was for comic relief. He seemed so impervious to ridicule that Emily couldn't help wondering if off-screen he smashed china and jabbed people.

"He's made a pretty good living for himself, Danny has," Mr. Macdonald said approvingly. He didn't mention Damien.

They were in grade ten when Damien made a move. Walking home from school together, Damien would suddenly take her hand and hold it in his. She didn't want to hurt his feelings, so she never told him she didn't want this. Instead she tried to remember to keep both hands wrapped around her books. She pretended not to notice where he had written D loves E on his book covers.

They had been to a high school dance together, Emily in a blue bengaline dress out of the catalogue, a step up from her mother's dreadful sewing, Damien in Danny's navy blue blazer, the sleeves of which were inches too short for his long arms. Like the other pairs of stick figures, they moved two steps sideways, one back, across the gym floor, the crêpe paper streamers pulled into a tent above their heads. She was safe enough here.

The time he picked to kiss her was walking home afterwards along the back streets, where the lampposts were widely spaced and there were tunnels of murky air between them. It was a tender kiss; his lips were soft, insistent. He put his hands on either side of her head, tilting it back. Tilting her gently. Beneath her feet, the ground shifted dangerously, and she ducked down. His hands held her, cupped warm on her shoulders.

"Don't be scared," he said. "I would never hurt you." He bent forward to kiss her again, eyes closed.

This time Emily got away. She ran through the tunnelled air, hair flying, mouth agape.

Behind her she heard him call, "Don't. Don't run."

At the corner, where there was light, she glanced back and saw Damien two street lights away, hands in his pockets, slouching along, letting her go.

After that, she started getting up earlier in the mornings and driving to school with her parents. She waited for them after school so she wouldn't meet Damien. If there was homework, she sent it over with Megan.

Peggy Roscoe passed by her on the street without speaking. Though she'd quit school, Peggy still had a girlfriend in grade twelve, so the news was out — Emily was stuck up. She thought she was too good for Damien.

This was partly true. Emily thought Damien should have been made of sterner stuff, that he shouldn't have given up so easily. When he got a steady girlfriend a few months later, she disowned ever having known him. She left Sydney Mines when she was seventeen, determined to disown it too.

For a long time after she'd moved away, she went so far as to lie about having lived in Sydney Mines. If someone asked her about where she'd grown up, she'd say Cape Breton. If pressed she'd say, in a vague sort of way, a small place near Sydney, you wouldn't know it. She felt ashamed of this now.

Sydney Mines hadn't changed much since she'd left; it was still the same size. But her perception of the landscape had changed. It wasn't monochromatic grey, as she had remembered it, but blatantly technicolour. It seemed every colour on the paint charts had been used. The town hall was teal blue, the school forest green, the churches robin's egg blue, moss green, maroon. Down here, near the mine, the houses looked like brightly painted codfish boxes strung along lengths of rope tossed overboard into a sea of green scrub. Some of the streets had houses on one side only. Here and there, front steps hadn't been built, deliberately cutting off access to the parlour, preserving the sanctity of carpeting and colour TV. Yards were treeless; trees here did not do well. There was no protection against the winter wind that swept off the ice floes in Cabot Strait.

Emily wondered if Damien lived down here somewhere. She knew he'd sold the big house next door. Her mother had mentioned that years ago in a letter. When Emily had written back asking where did he go, her mother's reply was that she'd no idea, he might have moved off the island altogether for all she knew.

Emily doubted that. He'd left leaving too late. Probably he'd become one of those Cape Bretoners who couldn't leave, who believed this island, this rock of red cliffs and green hills, was God's country. Maybe it was to catch God's eye that they used so much bright paint.

As she sat on the bench, Emily imagined what it would be like bumping into Damien. Coincidentally, of course. She'd ask him about his family. He'd married early, her mother had said, there were four kids close together. Maybe she'd go home with him. Have tea. She might even talk him into singing something for her. She'd keep the conversation light. There would be no mention of the past. She couldn't tell him now — any more than she could then — that her running away had to do not with him but with her father. He wouldn't remember anyway. Her wanting to see Damien had to do with knowing she'd disowned him, of living that down. She wanted to do this even though she knew that this

From a High Thin Wire

was an indulgence that, more than anything else, made her a tourist in Sydney Mines.

"What's Damien doing now?" She finally came out and asked because Mr. Macdonald hadn't said a word about him. She was beginning to think he was deliberately avoiding the subject, but when he answered, she thought she understood why.

"He's retired," Mr. Macdonald said, "same as the rest of us."

Emily knew retired meant laid off, *unemployed*. Had Damien become another hospitalized war veteran, spending winter in thermostatically-controlled rooms, summer warming himself on a sunny bench at the minehead, watching tourists like herself? Or had he found other things to do, organized a choir perhaps?

"You just might see him around," Mr. Macdonald said. "He comes down here sometimes if the weather's nice. If I see him, I'll tell him you were asking for him."

Another miner came up. Rotund and ruddy-cheeked and, she guessed, bald beneath his hard hat, he reminded her of Danny Roscoe. "The tour's starting," he said to her. "You'd better come with me."

"Isn't that just like an O'Hara?" Mr. Macdonald said. "Always thinks the women are after him."

"Listen to that, would you!" O'Hara turned to Emily. "These Scotchmen think they own the whole island. Talk about hogs."

Mr. Macdonald adjusted his bow tie. "If he gives you any trouble, you just report him to me."

Inside, there was more of the same. Emily presented her ticket, but O'Hara waved it away. She jammed the ticket into her jeans pocket, hooked her jacket onto one of the gaffs hanging from the shed beams and went into the room where they stored the gear. There, another miner, much younger than O'Hara, was handing out flashlights. When he went to strap on Emily's, O'Hara took the flashlight from him and fastened the belt around her waist so that the battery hung just above her hip. Then he looped the cord over her shoulder so she could manoeuvre the flashlight in front. He fiddled with the cord, making sure it was the right length. The other miner stood there grinning, leaning one elbow against the shelf.

"What a way with women you have, O'Hara," he said.

"Jealousy will get you nowheres."

"I'm not jealous. I'm full of admiration. I'm just standing here hoping to pick up a few pointers."

O'Hara put a red poncho over Emily's shoulders. "It'll keep you clean."

And a hard hat. "Regulations. You wouldn't want to hit your head on a tie."

"Hey, O'Hara, don't take all night," one of the miners yelled. "We got seven others ready to go down."

Besides the two men, students they looked like, there was a family of five, three school-aged daughters and their parents, campers, probably on their way to the Cabot Trail. O'Hara picked up a pointer and indicated the elevator. They got on; the door clanked shut, and they started down. The elevator was an open cage with grey metal bars, badly rusted. Water dripped off the sides of the shaft; Emily heard it splashing below.

The elevator cage thudded to the bottom. The door grated open. It was black, cold and wet.

"Put your flashlights on and follow me. Watch the water," O'Hara said; he was all business now.

Flashlights on, they followed O'Hara past puddle water. At the entrance to a tunnel, O'Hara stopped. "This mine goes six miles under the sea, 2,360 feet down to be exact, but we're only going to 680. We'll be following the rail line. Keep your heads down and watch your step. She drops a foot every ten feet, so we'll be walking on a slant."

There were dim lights strung out at intervals along the tunnel, and as they bent over, crab-walking the ties, Emily was able to see that the mine walls were shored up with heavy timbers and iron ties irregularly spaced. The whole mass had been sprayed with white powder to retard fire. The yellow lights and white powder gave a sulphurous thickness to the air.

From a High Thin Wire

They came out of the tunnel to a higher-ceilinged cave that was an intersection where the main tunnel plunged down and a smaller tunnel went off to a coal seam. O'Hara took them into the room where the engine controlled the cable drum, the cable that ran the coal cars to the tunnel bottom and back up. There were WARNING and DANGER signs pasted on the walls, large numbered instructions.

"This is the most important piece of equipment in the mine," O'Hara said. "Used to be up on top. But, after the accident, she was moved down here."

"What accident?" one of the daughters wanted to know.

"Cable broke. Fourteen men were killed."

Mr. Roscoe was in one of the cars that was cut off, racing out of control, plummeting down the tunnel, gathering speed, down, down, the sulphurous walls flashing past, stomachs sucked out, chests ripped open, eyes squeezed shut on inner darkness, the last chilling minutes careening past.

Despite Mr. Roscoe's temper, the Anglican church couldn't hold all the miners who came to the funeral. Emily went with her parents. She remembered her father saying the music would have made the old boy proud. Although Danny had come home for the funeral, it was Damien who sang the Twenty-third Psalm. He was eighteen then, and his voice had come out of the change a tenor.

Outside the engine room, Emily caught sight of a grey stag's head. It was lumpily constructed and clumsily painted, with red spots for eyes and antlers too thick for realism, but there was no mistaking it was a stag's head.

O'Hara saw her looking at it. "Some of the men made that. Used grease from the machine. Sort of built it up with blobs that fell off. The leftovers, like. Did a good job, I'd say."

Emily stared at the eyes, hoping she would see pupil dots emerge and dilate so she could see inside the stag's head, to know there were pictures inside it: meadows open and green, maple groves, autumn sunshine, coloured leaves. But the eyes remained blank, painted shut with what looked like nail polish.

O'Hara was leading them into another tunnel. Hunched over, their hats bumping rock, they switched on their flashlights and followed. This tunnel didn't open up even when they reached the coal face, so they had to stay bent over while O'Hara explained things. Emily sat on her handbag.

"You couldn't have done that when the mine was operating or the rats would've crawled right up your pant legs," O'Hara said.

Below her jeans, the meat of Emily's tanned ankle was exposed, tender white against the black coal. She got up quickly.

O'Hara laughed. "Don't worry. When the men left, the rats left. But boys oh boys, when they were here, you had to look out. We tied string around our cuffs so they wouldn't crawl up our legs. When you opened up your lunch pail, you had to kick 'em off with your boot. I always went back to where the tunnel opens so I could eat standing up." Here the light bulbs were larger and closer together, so visibility was better. But the shadows were blacker. The light shone on the layered coal face, glittering like rats' eyes.

"This machine is what gets the coal out of the seam. See, it's got a jack to hold up the roof while it digs out the coal. It goes in so far, then moves sideways. We always used this. Never used a pick and shovel."

The machine had a huge round saw-toothed blade that rotated when O'Hara switched it on. The blade moved forward, chewing into the seam. Chunks of coal dropped easily, tumbling into a cart. A black cloud of coal dust puffed out. The noise, rolled into a hard-probing core, drilled into Emily's ears.

O'Hara switched off the machine and directed their attention to the coal cars. "With the machine doing the digging, we had a devil of a job keeping up with it. The empty cars kept moving in. We had to keep moving the full ones out. Had to be quick about it, or you'd jam your hand."

That was what happened to Danny Roscoe. After the old man

From a High Thin Wire

was killed, there was nothing to keep him out of the mine. But he'd only worked down here a few months when he jammed his right hand between two cars. Broke the bones. Pulped them to sausage meat. It didn't show on the television screen. Danny had become skilful at keeping it behind his back or tucked inside his jacket front against his chest, as if he really was singing those true-blue love songs from his heart.

Damien quit grade twelve after that to work in the mine. There was no other money coming in. Peggy had married a farmer and moved to Margaree Harbour. It was a year before Danny's hand healed and he was able to get a job with a pickup band playing Saturday night dances. Even then he wasn't paid much, and there was Megan to get through school.

"You want some coal for souvenirs, this is your chance," O'Hara said. He took out plastic bags and handed them round.

Emily couldn't imagine a piece of coal as a souvenir. What was it a souvenir of, anyway? Would they be handing out jars of tar sand and oil someday? In Emily's view, handing out coal as a memento somehow cheapened the risk in getting it.

But O'Hara didn't seem to mind. He was helping the little girls load up their bags.

Emily's back ached from bending over. How did the men stand it, hunched over all day in the cold and damp? She straightened up and her plastic hard hat hit metal. She looked up and saw it had hit a horseshoe nailed to a beam.

After Emily had moved out West, her mother used to send her the *Cape Breton Post*, tied up in brown paper and string, third-class mail. Sometimes it was months before she looked through the pile of papers, and then it was only a quick glance before throwing them out. But she read every word of the cave-in. Clipped out the front page and folded it into her photo album. Eight men were trapped. Six days, no food, water, fresh air, the coal wedged tight around them. One of the men, it had to be an Irishman, was quoted as saying he knew they'd be rescued because there was a horseshoe nailed to a beam, they could feel it in the dark. Another miner, an Englishman, said it was Damien singing to them that kept their spirits up. Down there in the dark, he said, Damien sounded like a nightingale. There was a photograph of Damien on the front page. He looked old, haggard, his eyes staring whitely from blackened skin. He looked like someone returned from the dead.

There was a last stop in the mine tour, at the tipple that dumped the coal cars onto the conveyor belt that took the coal out, before O'Hara had them riding the cars up the long slope to the surface, the fresh air rushing down to meet them. At the top, they took off their gear and returned it to the shed.

Emily stepped outside to blinding July sunlight, to the plaintive wail of bagpipes. A girl in a kilt and knee socks was playing "Road to the Isles." Behind her unrolled a tartan of green swamp and blue sea, the water woven through with yellow threads.

Mr. Macdonald was waiting for her. Beside him was a tall man, badly stooped, with a polka-dot ascot at his neck. Damien. Just when she was beginning to wonder if she should ask Mr. Macdonald where he lived. He looked old, a paler version of the miner in the photograph. Without the coal dust and with his hair turned white, he no longer looked like his father's paper cut-out but the silhouette surrounding it.

"This is the fellow you were asking about," Mr. Macdonald said unnecessarily.

Emily took a step forward and stuck out a nervous hand. "Do you remember me? I used to live next door to you."

He looked so aged Emily thought he might have forgotten her. But he didn't. He took her hand, squeezing the fingers hard.

"How are you, Damien?" she said.

Damien smiled. He wore dentures, she noticed, and had shrinkage lines on his upper lip. The lips, thin now, pulled back, and a faint *f* came out. A voiceless *f*. An *f* squeezed out and shaped by a wheeze of air.

"He says he's fine," Mr. Macdonald interpreted.

But Emily didn't get it right away. It didn't register fast enough. Both men must have seen the disbelief on her face.

Mr. Macdonald helped her out. "Damien had an operation two years ago. Had his voice box removed. A plastic one put in. He's doing pretty good with it, wouldn't you say?"

Emily stood there holding Damien's hand, unable to let go of it, unable to speak.

So Mr. Macdonald went on. "These Welshmen are terrible fellas. Stubborn as mules. You wouldn't believe how stubborn they are. You can't get rid of one no matter how hard you try."

But even with Mr. Macdonald's help, Emily couldn't say what she wanted to say. What she wanted to say, now that he was finally in front of her, was: *I loved you, Damien. Once, a long time ago, I really loved you.* But there was a risk in saying this even to herself. The risk was not that Damien would be indifferent to this admission or think her guilty of foolish exaggeration, but that it might be mistaken for pity.

"He may have trouble speaking," Mr. Macdonald was prodding her, "but he has no trouble listening."

Slowly, with her other hand, Emily took the crumpled ticket out of her jeans pocket and held it up for Damien to see. "Look," she said, staring at it. "I bought a ticket. I must say it seemed strange buying a ticket. I mean, to go down and see the place where you and your father and brother worked. They sell tickets to all sorts of things nowadays, don't they?" She was babbling, she knew, trying too hard. "Would you believe just last week in Calgary, I bought a ticket . . ." She looked up then to engage Mr. Macdonald, but he had walked quietly away. She wanted to run after him. She felt a tightening around her hand. There was a wheezing sound.

Emily looked at Damien's mouth. She saw his tongue curl up-ward. She felt the soft explosion of air against her cheek. She watched the lips funnelling a *d*. The *d*, disembodied — separate from Damien — floated past her ear. "Don't run," he was saying.

The "away" was indiscernible, gulped down with an intake of air. But the next words were distinct enough; a *t* exploded. "This time," he said, and grinned. Then, with a gentlemanly grace which, Emily remembered, he had always possesed, even in his own parlour, he indicated a bench they could sit on.

They talked about their families, people they had both known, the energy crisis, the weather. Though Damien kept smiling and nodding, wheezing unselfconsciously, and the summer sun warmed the lobster-red bench where they sat, Emily could not tear her mind from the dark tunnels below. She wanted to go back down the mine, pry out the nails, bring the horseshoe up here and to hurtle it skyward, but it was such a pitiful, useless tool for smashing the eye of God.

Her Father's Daughter

By the time she was fifteen, Emily was used to going places with her father. To church mostly. Her father's churchgoing wasn't the result of religious conviction. In fact he referred to it as touring. And what country are we touring tonight, he'd say while they had high tea, a Sunday ritual, one of her mother's concessions to her father's Englishness. Though he seemed to be letting Emily make the choice in the guise of encouraging her independence, he wasn't really, because he refused to enter some churches. The Presbyterian and Baptist were blacklisted for their hell-fire and damnation sermons, and as principal of the Protestant elementary school, attending the Catholic church was unthinkable. That would be invading enemy territory. In Sydney Mines, you were either Protestant or Catholic, heathen or mick, free or enslaved. Though anyone living in that town haphazardly built over a labyrinth of mined-out tunnels might wonder if freedom to worship had actually been gained in the Atlantic crossing, or whether religious differences hadn't become more entrenched. Emily's mother claimed the Scots in Cape Breton were more Presbyterian than they had ever been in Scotland, the English more Anglican, the Irish more Catholic. The one thing they had in common, she said, was their ability to dig in their heels. Emily's father agreed, observing that, once the settlers found the new land too harsh for real spring, they fastened themselves to rocky crevasses like stubborn snails that even the wildest sea gales couldn't dislodge.

Emily and her father shuttled between the United and Anglican churches, neither of which Emily found satisfying. She went through the motions because it was a chance to be alone with her father, and she believed him when he told her she might get carried away without him — he was referring to her earlier longing to be Catholic, to that time when she'd gone to the Catholic church alone and seen the plaster Jesus move on the wooden cross. She found the United church insipid by comparison. There were no statues, rosaries, incense. The minister never looked anyone in the eye but stared fixedly over the congregation's heads, droning on incomprehensibly. Even her father didn't know what the minister was trying to say. He preferred the Anglican church, where the minister made no real effort to preach but strung together amusing anecdotes from the old country. Her father especially liked the boy soprano who sang the evensong solo. He compared him to a thrush singing in the green sward of a darkening churchyard. Her father said poetic things like that coming and going from church. Even though he was a principal, he still taught grade six history and English. He often quoted poetry and sang. Since he seldom did either in front of her mother, Emily took this as an indication that he was more himself when he was with her. It encouraged her belief that she had more in common with her father's side of the family than her mother's. Her mother's were stocky, square-jawed farmers, Danish-German hybrids. Practical, energetic, down-to-earth people. Emily much preferred her father's family, as she imagined them to be.

She didn't have much to go on. She'd never been to England, had never met her uncle or her grandfather. In any case, her grandfather had remarried and started another family, and all she had to rely on was her dead grandmother's picture, which was in an oval frame on her father's dresser. Her grandmother had a delicately boned face, small pointed chin and sad brown eyes. She was wearing a high-necked blouse with a brooch pinned on the lace. Her brown hair was piled on top of her head in a soft mounding; it looked like a single pin could be pulled out and her hair would come tumbling down. Emily was growing her own hair and tying it up in rags at night so that it would look tumbled like her grandmother's. She knew she was too thin and too awkward to be considered as beautiful as the woman in the photograph, but after she'd started doing up her hair, her father tweaked a curl one day and told her she reminded him of his mother so she thought a metamorphosis was possible one day.

When her father had pulled her hair that day, Emily wanted to touch his hair where it curled, clumsily barbered behind his ears. She wanted to tell him that she liked his greying hair, that its scruffiness was part of his charm, that he seemed to be growing younger every day. Not like her mother, who was getting older and thicker, preoccupied with marking workbooks and getting meals on time. Emily knew her mother wouldn't tell her father how handsome he was; she was more inclined to bully him into a second helping to put meat on his bones. Her parents seldom said nice things to each other, at least not in front of Emily. They seldom touched each other, let alone her.

But stuck in her memory was a picture of her father at the beach once when she was ten and they had dug a deep hole together near the shore where the sand was soft. After they had dug down three feet, they made a tunnel big enough for her father to sit in with his legs straight out. He was in that position when a wave came in unexpectedly and splashed him. He started shivering and was hugging himself when Emily came up behind him and, wrapping her hot, sandy body around his, rocked him gently. He liked it, she could tell, because he put his hands on her arms and held her there. After a while, he wriggled out of the hole and piggybacked her into the water, where he dumped her into the cold waves, then ran, laughing, back to her mother, who was reading near the dunes.

Every once in a while, five or six Saturdays a year, Emily's father took it into his head to visit the moonshiner. Her mother didn't approve of this, or his heavy smoking, but she didn't openly express disapproval. Even if Emily's father tried to bait her mother with barbed sarcasms about having a country hick for a wife, her mother would go about the house without saying much. There might be a "Now, now, James" or a "Don't be unkind" tossed off in the same encouraging way she talked to her grade three class. These mild urgings usually made her father more sarcastic. Sometimes he would shout at her mother, trying to rouse her fury to match his, but this only resulted in his being defeated by a coughing fit and a retreat to his study, the spare room upstairs.

This was also his retreat when he got home from the moonshiner's. He took the bottle upstairs, locked the door and didn't reappear until Sunday noon, by which time he would be bleary-eyed and morose. Still wearing pyjamas and bathrobe, holding onto the banister, he got himself down to the kitchen to make a pot of tea. Carrying the tea upstairs, he drank the entire potful while he marked compositions. The air was blue with horrified remonstrations about the illiteracy of his students, and he punished himself by reading out examples of the most hopeless cases.

Late Saturday, when he was well into his toot, as he jocularly referred to it afterwards, he sang, sometimes so loudly they could hear him downstairs at the supper table. There was nothing jocular about his singing.

When true hearts lie withered
And fond ones have flown,

O, who will inhabit
This bleak world alone?

Besides "'Tis the Last Rose of Summer," he sang all the other sad songs he could think of: "Loch Lomond," "Danny Boy," before moving on to the dreary ballads: "Lucy Grey," "Bonny George Campbell," "Barbara Allan."

When he was eighteen, Emily's father had left England for Canada. This was after his mother died and bequeathed him a small inheritance, which was enough to put himself through normal college in Fredericton, where he met Emily's mother, who was there on an IODE bursary. They got married and went north to teach, earning enough money to finance four years at university. All this was before Emily was born. The songs her father sang were so sad that Emily was convinced that he had to get drunk sometimes because he couldn't bear the pain of mourning his mother. Her own mother's practicality, her outward acceptance of these "wakes," as she called them, reinforced this view. Your father's on one of his wakes, she would say as she carried the kitchen chairs into the dining room, it's a good time to scrub the floor while he's out of the way. She usually managed to get the pantry, hall and bathroom floors done as well.

Her mother wasn't a particularly good housekeeper; she cleaned house the way she sewed clothes, in sudden gusts of energy, as if an unexpected storm, a big wind had gotten up outside and, shut up as she was, she might as well make the most of it. Nor would she waste time driving to the moonshiner's. It was Emily who got to go with her father.

As soon as they got into the car, Emily's father started quoting poetry, Shakespeare. He knew *Macbeth* off by heart and on a long drive like today would start with the witches on the heath, work his way through the castle to Forres, back to the castle, then down to England, ending up finally in Dunsinane.

The moonshiner's was up highland way which meant they had to leave home after breakfast and didn't get back until after lunch. Emily didn't question why they went so far to find a bootlegger, or why her father didn't buy liquor in Sydney Mines. She thought it was because of the scenic drive. Past the lake shining blue and gold in the sunlight. Across on the flat-bottomed ferry that held their car and three others. On the other side of the lake, the land got hillier, and there were grazing sheep, grey barns, rail fences. Her father took a narrow gravel road that wound past bushes scratching dust off the sides of the car. Here the land was browner, scrubbier, too poor for sheep. They came to an orchard where only a few trees had green leaves on them; the rest were dead, bare-limbed. They looked like oversized pieces of driftwood stuck here for artistic effect. Though who would bother with artistic effect in this rundown, neglected neck of the woods?

Her father stopped the car beside a weathered barn standing at an angle as if blown into that position by a persistent winter wind. Down in the hollow beside a dried-up brook with a board across it was a small house, also grey. It was toward this house that her father walked. "You stay here," he said, before he got out of the car. Emily had no particular desire to get out. There was nothing here that interested her and it was hot. She leaned her head against the seat back and closed her eyes.

Where had the old man been when they arrived? Did they drive past him and not see him standing there? Or did he hear the car door slam and come from the loft, down the steps built on the outside of the barn? Couldn't he see that her father wasn't there, that he had gone to the house for him? She didn't hear him come up. Her arm was crooked over the rolled-down window. The old man's hand was on her bare skin before she knew he was there. The skin of his hand was brown and wrinkled, and his claw-curved nails had dirt underneath.

She wasn't afraid of him at first, only startled by his ugliness. She had never been this close to such a repulsive-looking man. He stuck his face through the window so that she was staring into a pair of watery, pink-rimmed eyes whose whites looked as if they'd been injected with red ink. His head was bald and peeling, his chin brown and scrubby as the field they had passed. He opened his mouth in a grin. Because he was toothless, she couldn't be certain that it was a grin — later she came to think of it as a leer. It was only when the strong odour of sour, vinegary breath blew warm into her nostrils that she eased toward the centre of the car seat. His hand moved from her arm to her hair whose curls were looped into a ponytail that fell forward over her shoulder and down her breast.

"Such pretty hair," he crooned. Emily was surprised by the softness of his voice, which didn't fit with the rest of him. "The wife had the same hair. Brown as a mare's tail." He laughed, pink gums showing. "My, but you're a nice young filly."

His hand left her hair and reached boldly for her breast. It was a quick, greedy gesture — he would settle for this rough handling, knowing it was all he would get.

Emily got behind the wheel. As she retreated, his hand slapped her thigh where it was bare beneath her shorts. Then he went around to the driver's side. Emily moved to the middle. If he tried to get in, she'd open the opposite door and run for her father.

"Hey, Mac!" she heard her father call. "I've been looking for you."

The old man turned away indifferently, his brown hand dropping from the window as if he was discarding an apple he'd bitten into and found too sour.

While her father followed the moonshiner up the flimsy stairs to the barn loft where the still was kept, Emily sat, her hands balled into tight indignant fists. The old coot. Lecher. She knew the word from her mother. How dare he. Ugly, he was so ugly you couldn't believe he was human. Imagine him mauling her like that. Dirty old man. She sat there, back rigid, legs tightly crossed at the knees, reviling him, unable to admit, because of his grotesqueness and the suddenness of the attack, that some secret part of her had liked the touch of his hand.

Her mother had warned her about dirty old men. And sex.

She did it by taking her to a show that ran one week at the Strand Theatre. The first show was for females only. You were supposed to be sixteen to get in, but Emily's mother told a white lie, knowing the ticket seller, who had once been a pupil of hers, would never question her honesty. Inside, the concession counter lights were turned off, the popcorn machine shut down. If further evidence of the gravity of the situation was needed, a white-uniformed nurse stood at the head of each aisle. The theatre was packed, people had come from miles around, so Emily and her mother had to sit near the front.

There were three movies. The first was entitled *Mother and Daughter*. It was about a sixteen-year-old girl named Joan who met a dashing air force pilot in his mid-twenties and let him drive her home from the school dance in his convertible. They parked. She let him go all the way. You didn't see it happening, you just knew from the way the two heads slid down out of sight behind the car seat like twin suns dipping to the horizon. Emily got no more satisfaction out of it than she did from her geography text which reported the sun to be coming up on the other side of the world — she had to take someone else's word for it. Joan's parents were rich and civilized, so she had trouble telling them she was pregnant and took half a bottle of pills rather than admit the truth. Her mother found her on the bathroom floor, but they got her stomach pumped out in time. She had to go away to have the baby, to cut down on the disgrace.

The second movie was old stuff. Emily had seen it all in the book her mother had deliberately left on the end table in the living room. There were diagrams of male and female organs, seeds and semen, fetuses and birth. Emily had never seen a real male organ. Her father was fastidiously modest, not like her mother, who wandered around upstairs in her bra and panties, unconcerned about her spreading thighs and varicose veins. She was the only one in her family to get a university education and seemed satisfied with that, relegating vanity, primping, fussing over clothes and figure to her sisters. It was left to Emily's imagination what a penis, the word her mother used, looked like; it seemed entirely possible to get into trouble without seeing one.

The third film was where it was expected you might faint and the nurses would carry you out. It was a barrage of photographs. These were real enough, the effects of syphilis and gonorrhea. Hideously deformed babies, swollen penises, raw, bleeding labia were magnified on the screen. Naked people lined up for inspection like arrested criminals so others could see their scabs, the running sores all over their bodies. According to the doctor narrating the film, these diseases were everywhere. They were highly contagious. Emily thought there were probably people walking around Sydney Mines who had this sort of thing beneath their clothing.

When the movie was over and Emily and her mother went outside into the night, Emily thought they had walked into a bizarre crowd assembled to watch a fire, but it was only the red light of the theatre marquee flashing above the lineup of people: men in twos and threes solidly packed to the corner. The show they were to see was the same except the first movie was entitled *Father and Son*. There didn't seem to be many sons in the lineup, mostly men. Some of the miners grinned at the women walking past, their teeth white against coal-tanned skin.

It wasn't the movie but Emily's mother who had the last word about sex. As they were walking home from the theatre, her mother said, "What I want you to remember about sex is that it's not worth risking pregnancy for. When the time comes for you to go out with boys, you'll have to be careful or you'll get yourself into an awful mess. You need a strong sense of self-preservation."

This was only her mother's opinion. What Emily saw more clearly was that not everyone wanted a strong sense of self-preservation. For instance, her old friend, Petra Commeau, was pregnant, and she didn't seem scared or ashamed. Emily met her on the street in front of Leong's Café where Petra quit grade eight to waitress. She was too big to work now; the cotton of her skirt showed through the gaps where her sweater was buttoned over her belly. The baby was coming any day now, Petra said, and Emily noticed greenish scum on her teeth. Did she have one of those awful diseases inside her pants? Would the baby be hideously deformed? The baby would be company for her new baby brother, Petra was saying, they'd be like twins. She was leaving the baby with her mother and going to Halifax afterwards because her boyfriend was in the Navy. No matter how hard Emily stared at Petra's swollen belly, she couldn't make the connection between this woman and the girl she used to wait for after school so they could play together. The only thread she could follow, one that thickened, eventually taking on more significance, roping off their two families, was remembering how Petra often talked about being wakened up in the middle of the night by the noise of her parents doing it, whereas the only evidence Emily had of her parents' coupling was herself. Since her mother had an operation and couldn't have any more children, there was no way of telling. There was no point in asking. Emily understood that her mother had taken her to the movie rather than explain things herself. And her mother had an offhand way of deflecting questions she didn't want to answer. When Emily asked her what she thought of Petra's being pregnant, her mother skirted the issue; she merely said the poor girl hadn't had much of a chance.

Not like Emily's father, who denounced Petra as a trollop. He wasn't surprised by her pregnancy; she'd probably been rolling about in the bushes for years, and Emily had been too naïve to realize it. He approved of Heather Stewart, who was still chaste. Heather's parents had packed her off to a private girl's school for safekeeping, but Emily saw her on holidays when they went to softball games. Sometimes after a game, she and Heather allowed two ballplayers to walk them home. They even accepted a chocolate bar or a bottle of pop bought at Dirty Dan's. But they never let the ballplayers walk them home separately. They hadn't missed the elaborate way the boys flashed the French safes when they opened up their wallets to pay for the treats.

Emily also kept her distance from Wilfred Brogan, a red-faced man with a bowler hat and a long, black coat unbuttoned even in

From a High Thin Wire

winter, who sometimes peered in their window. He was an alkie who lived in a shack near Greener's Cliff. It was always night time when Wilf looked in their window, standing on the flowerbed staring into the dining room, his black bulky shape outlined against the snow. He'd come along the beach once summers ago when Emily and Petra were swimming below the cliff. They saw him fiddling with his fly and got out of there fast.

"He's just a dirty old man looking for encouragement," her mother told her. "It's the same with any of these lechers. They just want attention. They're pathetic, really."

When Emily's father was on one of his toots, he usually slept in the spare room, not in his twin bed beside her mother's. Emily's room also had twin beds. The second bed was where her mother laid out her sewing patterns for cutting or left piles of mending where she wouldn't be reminded by the sight of them. Now the bed was covered with wool sweaters laid out to dry on newspapers and brown paper.

It was the crackling of the newspapers that woke her. That and her father's singing. He had pushed open her door and the hall light shone on the other bed so Emily could see him plainly. He was lying on his back in his pyjamas, knees up, hugging himself as if he were cold. He was rocking back and forth on top of the sweaters, warbling plaintively like an overgrown wingless bird unable to leave its nest.

Rock-a-bye baby,
On the treetop,
When the wind blows,
The cradle will rock . . .

Seeing her father in this position, stripped of his defences, so openly wanting love, filled Emily with pity and disgust. The pity was for her father, the disgust was for her mother. Why didn't her

---

Her Father's Daughter

mother give him more love? Why did she insist on twin beds? Her mother had said it was because he snored, but Emily knew it was because her mother was cold. Frigid was the word. She had picked up the word from Heather, who had used it to describe the school headmistress.

Emily wondered if she should go over and put her arms around him.

Midway through the third round of the lullaby, her father got up off the sweaters, swinging his long legs to the floor, deftly for one so drunk, and came toward Emily's bed. The suddenness of this movement instinctively made her edge closer to the wall.

Her father came down on her bed, crawling forward onto the blankets on his knees, then rolling on his side in fetal position, facing Emily; one arm flopped across her. "Hold me," he mumbled. "Hold me." Emily caught a whiff of his breath, as sour and vinegary as the moonshiner's. She turned to the wall. Her father's hand went round her waist. "Hold me," he mumbled again, "hold me," like a hurt child needing his mother. Emily was overwhelmed by the knowledge that her father had come to her for love. She rolled over onto her back, her father's hand a dead weight on her. With knees bent and heels dug into the mattress, she pushed herself up so that her father's head was on her breast. She put her hand on his hair, stroking where it curled over his ears. "There, there," she whispered.

Her father's hand came up onto her breasts, kneading them gently, fingering their roundness, soft as jellyfish. Purple threads shot out of her breasts into her belly. They wound around and around each other, their tips probing, making secret hollows and caves in her flesh. She felt she was dark inside, tunnelled out and full of water, and the swaying tentacles were exploring the watery darkness. Her father's hand kept moving; Emily closed her eyes; her eyelids seemed to be floating.

Then, as abruptly as he'd come to her bed, her father's hand flopped onto the sheet, and Emily felt herself sinking. The purple threads became rigid. She nudged her father's head closer to the breast, wanting his hand again, but his mouth opened and he began to snore. Still she kept mothering him, patting him on the head.

He began to get heavy. Her breast throbbed, she thought it was from the weight of his head. She began to ease herself away, gently, so she wouldn't wake him. She put her hands on either side of his head, cradling it, sliding it onto the pillow, but as soon as her hands closed on his cheeks, his eyes opened. He looked at her and grunted.

"Oh, it's you," he said and rolled onto the floor; it was as ordinary a movement as a rolling pin falling off a kitchen counter.

There was no mistaking the disappointment in his eyes. Who had he expected to see if not her?

After he had swayed into the hallway, she heard him open the door to the bedroom across the hall, where her mother was sleeping. She heard him say something and her mother mumble drowsily; probably she was telling him to go to bed. Her father had left both doors open and the hall light on. By leaning sideways off the bed, Emily could see straight into her parents' room; she could see her father had crawled into bed with her mother, that he had his arm around her waist. It was only then that it occurred to her that he had mistaken the twin bed in her room for her mother's.

She got up and slammed the door shut, then shoved the dresser in front of it in case her father should return — she still had to believe in that possibility. She lay on the bed, her fists thrust hard against her belly trying to bruise the flesh, to loosen a chip of bone, a particle of grit that would grow a shell.

In the morning, she got up early to go to church. Her mother was already up working at report cards at the kitchen table. Emily ignored her. It was all very well to take her to a movie and give her a book to read, but her mother hadn't told her the most important thing about sex, which was that she and Emily's father still did it.

She chose the Presbyterian church. While Reverend Mac-Ginnis shouted about the weaknesses of the flesh, Emily listened, inwardly trembling. She couldn't hear enough of it. When she got home, she thumbed through the Old Testament looking for any reference at all to sex, but there wasn't much besides the begats, the concubines and the burning condemnations of incest.

Her father never mentioned that night and seemed anything but pathetic.

Emily had trouble being civil to either of her parents. She made unreasonable demands and didn't disagree with them when they remarked that they had spoiled her. They'd tried not to, but with an only child — here they sighed as if the burden of raising her was interminable — maybe with an only child it was inevitable. Emily took the last three grades in two years so she could get through faster and make her escape. She stopped going anywhere with Damien Roscoe, who lived next door and, until he kissed her, had been a friend. All this time a shell thickened around the particle of grit. It was an ugly shell, warty with marine encrustations.

Historical Fiction

When Emily Elizabeth Prentice made the leap from Sydney Mines High School to college, what she most feared was falling into the moat, a deep trench filled with sluggish water surrounding the castle. The moat was somewhat like the Emperor's new clothes; strictly speaking it wasn't there, yet Emily could see it plainly. And she could see the heads bobbing on its slimy surface. These were the heads of the social outcasts: the serious students, the unpopular and the unmarriageable; their crimes were branded on their foreheads for everyone to see: reading, frequenting the library, writing poetry, studying theology, soul searching, discussing absolute truths. From the beginning, Emily knew the moat must be avoided, that she must watch her step or risk stumbling into the curdled heads that coated the swill like grease. Once Emily strayed off the path and found herself staring at a brown-haired youth who lay on his back in the moat reading Plato. He was actually floating, his long body stretched out, knees bent to hold the book. When he saw Emily, he grinned lopsidedly. "Come on in," he called. "The water's warm." Emily hesitated but caught herself in time and hurried back to the castle.

After that, she was careful to keep to the pathways criss-crossing the lawns. The lawns sloped downward toward a small village where ordinary folk lived. Emily seldom saw these people because village and castle life remained separate, though occasionally a drunken knight besotted with unrequited love might charge down the hill and into the village tilting his lance at old women, children and dogs so that the sheriff would be compelled to lock him in a dungeon.

The castle was an ugly, red-bricked residence sheltering two hundred virgins and presided over by a witch who kept the keys to the large front doors and a doomsday book into which she wrote the misdemeanours, as well as the comings and goings of the virgins. The maidens were forever letting their hair hang from casement windows, discovering secret passageways, undressing in lighted windows with drapes undrawn. Keeping them chaste and dutiful was an insurmountable task, one requiring the witch's constant vigilance and her most powerful incantations. Her only assistants were the clergy, who seldom showed themselves outside the chapel, and a cat name Freud. Frood, the maidens called him as they stumbled over him in dark hallways. Freud knew the rooms in which the giddy virgins worshipped Cupid, drinking wine after curfew, lighting candles at the marriage altar. These rituals occurred when one of the virgins escaped long enough to betroth herself, returning to the castle with a diamond ring.

Emily Elizabeth Prentice had not been living in the castle for long when she was asked to attend one of these rituals — a diamond ring ceremony. She had the honour of sitting on a cushion just inside the door, the same cushion that had earlier been used to parade the ring around the chamber. The ceremony was presided over by the beautiful Irene. Gowned in white, Irene waved a magic wand over the betrothed's head while wearing the betrothed's ring to see how it sparkled on her own white hand. It was her intention to wave the wand over everyone in the room to bring her good fortune. The maidens were clamouring for this royal favour — it was rumoured that the beautiful Irene was soon to be crowned a princess in the Realm of the Engaged.

Because she was awaiting her turn by the door, Emily was the first to see the door handle move. "Look!" she cried and pointed. The girlish prattle ceased. All eyes latched onto the door handle, which was turning slowly, like a screw. Presently the door swung inward, and there stood the witch, carrying Freud and dressed in a long black robe, having changed from her daytime clothes in which she disguised herself as a psychology professor. She stepped into the room. "Who's the victim this time?" she cackled; the witch never could be funny.

The maidens tittered.

The witch's eye pounced on the diamond which glittered on Irene's graceful hand. Irene proffered her finger.

"It's Daphne's," Irene said.

The witch's eyes flicked from Irene's finger to the betrothed. She sighed again. "Well, perhaps it's the best thing for you, Daphne," she said, then added meanly, "Unless you can pull up your marks, you might be better off getting married."

This remark was entirely out of bounds. The maidens' rules of etiquette strictly forbade any mention of marks.

"It's a good thing it isn't *you*, Irene," the witch went on. "One of the conditions of your being allowed to return this year was that you study harder. You can't play and keep up with your studies at the same time."

"Oh but I intend to," Irene simpered. She fluttered her eyelashes and dimpled her chin. Under her breath, she muttered, "Not like you, you old bat." It was only when the witch looked away that Irene's mask dropped and she resembled Gretel getting ready to push the witch into the oven.

"Well, don't the rest of you girls get any ideas," the witch warned. "Remember you're here to study."

The virgins weren't here to study but to marry. The witch only pretended not to know this. It was a deception used to cover up her disappointment that she'd never had a man, that all she had to show for those years of college was a PhD. That was why she'd been forced to spend the lonely hours since sitting in ivy-covered rooms, spinning her hair in circles of disenchantment, gliding along dark corridors with Freud in her arms.

Freud watched the virgins through half-closed eyes.

"Come on, you sleepy sphinx," the witch said to him softly. With the virgins, she used another tone. "It's time for lights out," she snapped.

"Nosy old bitch!" Irene hissed as soon as the door closed. "Snooping around. She's only got one thing on her mind — how far you had to go to get your ring, Daphne. She wants to hear all the details spelled out, the dried-up prune. She's so frustrated she can't stand to see us have any fun. We'll get her for this. We'll do the dummy trick." She snapped her fingers. "Somebody get paper and pen."

One of the maidens thrust these at her. Irene took the paper and pen and crooked a finger at Emily. "Come here," she said. "I've got something for you to do."

Emily crawled off her cushion and was about to stand when Irene said, "Don't get up. You can write on the floor. I'll tell you what to put down." She handed Emily the paper and pen.

"*My Dear Agnes,*" Irene began. Emily knew Agnes was the witch's alias. "*I must forbid you to write me love letters.*" Irene dictated, her lovely eyes narrowed to slits. "*They have caused me much embarrassment and anger. As I have explained over and over, I do not love you. It is not because you are ugly and have a wart on your nose.* She does," Irene giggled, "she really does. *But because my heart has been given to someone else. I am afraid, Dear Agnes, you will have to find another man to take to your bed. Or satisfy yourself.*"

Dutifully, Emily wrote this down. She thought it was mean, but then so was the witch.

"When she goes to class, we'll slip into her apartment and rig up a dummy." Irene nodded at Emily. "You can come."

"But I have History 200," Emily protested.

"Skip it," Irene said.

Emily skipped it. The dummy was a man's shirt and trousers stuffed with pillows from the witch's bed. It was posed sitting at the witch's desk, pen in hand, composing the letter. While Irene and Daphne arranged the dummy, Emily kept an eye on the door. She needn't have bothered; this part of the castle was empty. Irene and Daphne seemed to know this and took their time. Daphne swiped one of the chocolate mints from the silver tea tray and gulped it down.

"Last year," Irene proclaimed loudly, "we put a dummy in her toilet cubicle with his shoes sticking out under the door so the witch thought a workman had wandered into her bathroom. It took her hours to catch on." Irene giggled. "Then, when she finally got in there, she peed on the floor because we had plastic wrap taped across the bowl."

As they were leaving the witch's apartment, Irene snapped an iron lock on Emily's wrist. "Since you were in my room last night after curfew, the witch might call you in for questioning. You don't tell, see? Not a word. The year before last, Ophelia blabbed and told who put the frog prince in the witch's bed. Told everything. Named names. She went mad afterwards," Irene said, "quite mad. Besides," she added, "there are rewards for being loyal."

Emily already knew that one of the rewards was a key to the laundry room door. The laundry room had a window which allowed the maidens to keep their trysts with knights. She also knew what had happened to Ophelia — she had drowned herself in the moat.

As Irene had predicted, Emily was summoned for an inquisition in the witch's office. Office, she called it, as if she really were a psychology professor. Irene had primed her, so Emily knew what to expect. Strapped to the hard chair, she listened to the witch trying to soften her up.

"You're a first-year student, and as with most of my first-year girls, I like to make sure they get off to a good start," the witch began. "Many girls who come here with good marks go astray in their first year. All these young men about," the witch cackled. "It's a big temptation."

Emily didn't fall for this.

"Some of the girls have trouble with the rules. But I tell them the rules are here for their own good." The witch paused.

"Yes," Emily replied. Irene had said *yes* and *no* were the pre-ferred answers. In the right places of course.

"I won't mention any names, but some girls here are a poor in-fluence. They have a negative attitude that is especially harmful to first-year girls." The witch leaned across the desk, resting her hairy chin on her hands. "I want you to know I'm here to help you. I have your best interests at heart."

Emily allowed another yes.

"And, in return, I expect you to respect my position. It wouldn't be wise to become involved in childish pranks. That sort of thing goes on around here from time to time."

Emily did not respond.

"Is there anything you want to tell me?" The witch sat back in her creaky chair, and waited.

This was the silent treatment Irene had warned her about. Sooner or later the witch got to this, asked the question and then sat back to wait, relying on virginal flightiness, Freud's self-satisfied purring and the ticking clock to force a confession.

Emily waited her out.

Until the witch finally said, with unnecessary testiness Emily thought, "All right then, you may go."

On All Hallows Eve, heroic knights assembled in the courtyard of the castle to woo the maidens with daring feats. The boldest smuggled a greased pig into the witch's apartment. Others tied a cow to the front door. Still others struggled to get a milk wagon across the drawbridge and up the hill. But the bravest knight of all was the one who rode the milkman's white steed. He was fair-haired, blue-eyed and handsome. His name was Sir Walter. He rode majestically around the courtyard beneath the windows. That was how Emily Elizabeth first met him. She was leaning out a casement window pouring water on the knights while others threw down their brassieres. When her water landed on Sir Walter's golden crown, he looked up and made eye contact.

It was also Sir Walter who led the November panty raid, when knights stormed the castle in the early morning hours while the witch slept and the virgins were getting dressed. Emily was just stepping into her panties when the blond knight burst into her room and tore the lacy underthings from her very hands. To Emily's dismay, her panties were returned the next day. She had hoped her flowered lace would be flying high on fortress walls all through the winter snows, a banner to spring's promises. Alas, her panties remained only panties because of the misguided intentions of Don Quixote, a knight errant who insisted on rounding up the stolen underwear and returning it to her himself, apparently thinking it would please her. He had read the label, *E. Prentice*, sewn into the waistband.

Don Quixote sat beside Emily in English 200. He was a tall, loose-jointed knight with brown hair and lopsided grin. Don Quixote took all kinds of foolish chances. For instance, he made no effort to cover up the fact that he was well read. He was careless enough to study in the main room of the library instead of hiding in the stacks. He made friends with all sorts of social outcasts: serious students, kitchen maids, theologues. Once he was even seen taking tea in the witch's apartment with a group of students reported to belong to, of all things, a psychology club.

At the pre-Christmas ball, Sir Walter was crowned Campus Prince. Emily Elizabeth was made a Lady-in-Waiting. This was a complete surprise. In Sydney Mines, she'd cloistered herself in churches and books; she hadn't known she was princess material. Since coming to the castle, she'd become an exotic flower sprung from the sea, one that was bending tentatively toward the light, its shell abandoned in another ocean. She did look somewhat like an emerging Venus, being slender-hipped and pale-fleshed, with soft dreamy eyes. When she danced, her long, brown hair swayed around her like floating sea grass. Prince Walter asked her to dance first, before Princess Irene. They danced with their eyes, not their feet, which kept tripping over the hem of Emily's borrowed gown.

After the ball, Emily attended a party held in Princess Irene's castle suite, two rooms under the eaves on the third floor, far away from the witch's apartment. The virgins, dressed in thick robes, hair brushed down, sat cross-legged on the floor gorging themselves on cold chicken, ham, pickles. Most of the food belonged to Princess Irene and was imported for the occasion. This sharing was a sign of royal blood. A Princess was expected to be generous, pleasant and friendly with everyone, no matter who they were. That was what being popular meant. With all the people at the party, it was a wonder she found time to talk to Emily, but she did. She did this most frankly. After graduation, she said, settling down beside Emily, she and Prince Walter were marrying, although he didn't know it yet. The only reason they weren't betrothed was because, like most knights, Prince Walter spent much of his time at the round table carousing and bragging about his exploits on the field. It was a point of honour with him, indeed he considered it his personal responsibility, to protect the maidenhead of every virgin who crossed his path, Emily Elizabeth included. She must not let his gallantry stifle her interest in other, and perhaps more suitable, swains.

Though Emily took this wise counsel to heart, she didn't refuse Prince Walter when he showed up at the castle and invited her out. Being fussed over and sought after, especially by a Prince, was so new to her, she wasn't ready to give it up. Emily Elizabeth and Prince Walter went out into the cold night air, the northern lights flashing over their heads like burnished swords. Hand in hand, they went down the hill and, together with the village folk, watched *Love Is a Many-Splendoured Thing*. Returning to the castle, after the movie, Prince Walter talked to her about his exploits on the jousting field. Had she seen him score the winning point in the November tournament? Yes she had. Actually she knew nothing of the tournament's rules and had been unable to follow the chargings up and down the field. The truth was the tournament had bored her just as talking about it now bored her. But she didn't know she was bored. She was too busy being a lady-in-waiting to realize this. Prince Walter asked if she was coming to watch the tournament on Friday night; it was a winter match where knights jousted on ice. "Don't put your name in the doomsday book," he said, and "I'll get you into the castle afterwards; just remember to leave a window open." Prince Walter knew all the witch's tricks, how she kept the maidens locked inside. In fact, he had donated his shirt and trousers for the dummy. Emily said yes, she'd go to the tournament and watch him. He kissed her then, the way she expected he would; it was a healthy first-night kiss, cold-nosed and athletic.

On Friday night, Emily put a perfume bottle under the bathroom window to keep it open and slipped out the front door when the monitor of the doomsday book wasn't looking. Inside the jousting tent, she sat beside Don Quixote and Sancho Panza. Sancho was a villager named Nigel, who worked in the pottery workroom of the Fine Arts building, cleaning up messes. It was risky being seen with someone like Sancho, but Emily thought she could afford it. She certainly couldn't sit alone. Don Quixote did not appear to notice when she sat down beside him. Emily would have thought he'd have shown pleasure to be seen beside a lady-in-waiting, but he was obviously ignorant of the rules of courtship. When Princess Irene filed in with her entourage, he said scornfully, "Here comes Her Royal Highness."

And when Irene had seated herself in front of them next to the boards and turned around to smile and wave, Don Quixote glared at her. "Does she never tire of smiling?" he muttered.

Sancho Panza's thick shoulders began to shake; apparently he thought this was some sort of joke.

But Emily was not amused. "What's wrong with smiling?" she said. As a lady-in-waiting, she considered it her duty to defend royalty.

When the players charged onto the ice, Prince Walter looked up and waved, not at Princess Irene, but at Emily.

"Well, well," Don Quixote said sarcastically. "It looks like you've caught the prince's fancy."

Emily blushed becomingly and confessed she was meeting the prince after the match.

The match began strongly enough. There was a drum roll during which the players stood, gloved hands at their sides, lance sticks at half-mast as they paid homage to the Queen. Then the precious rubber was dropped onto the ice and the knights began charging up and down, spearing and poking each other with their lance sticks whilst the rubber circle bounced from one end of the ice like a ball, scarcely ever going into the nets placed at either end for that purpose. It was rough and dangerous work with nobody seeming to get anywhere. Don Quixote kept muttering, making deprecating remarks about Walter, which distracted Emily. Midway through the tournament, Don Quixote stalked out in disgust, followed by Sancho Panza. This left Emily free to concentrate on watching Prince Walter, who spent most of the match making graceful circles and figure eights, unaware of the black rubber thing zinging dangerously past him. This suited Emily fine; she couldn't possibly keep track of the precious rubber *and* the prince. She wasn't even aware of Princess Irene's turnings about, giving her what could only be described as dirty looks.

Near the end of the tournament, Emily began to admit that she was just a little bit bored, but she managed to overcome the boredom by thinking about meeting Prince Walter afterwards. It was at this point — during the final seconds of the match — that the black rubber lifted off the ice, sailed over the boards and whacked Princess Irene squarely on top of her crown. The princess swooned backwards; fortunately there were enough in her entourage to catch her. Immediately, Prince Walter dropped his lance stick and hit the knight who had fired the offending rubber at the princess. The knight staggered backwards but soon regained his balance and punched the prince squarely in the nose. Blood spurted from the royal nostrils. The prince jammed his fist down his opponent's throat, breaking two teeth. In retaliation, the knight blackened Prince Walter's eye. While he had the advantage, the knight knocked the prince to the ice and kicked him soundly. For some time Walter lay there, perhaps longer than was necessary.

Finally he got up and, wiping his nose, he approached Irene, who by now had come to and was staggering toward him. Then, hand in hand, the two of them stumbled across the ice, allowing others to lead them out of the rink and to the hospital.

For some time, Emily sat alone in her seat. There were tears in her eyes such as one might expect to appear at the end of a romantic tale when two lovers so obviously destined for each other ride off into the sunset. Her tears were not for a happy ending, however, but for herself. She was angry at Walter. By starting a fight and getting himself hauled off to the hospital, he had left her stranded here with no way of getting back into the castle. As the rink lights were snapped off one by one, dropping her into darkness, the severity of this problem confronted her. She fled the rink just before the door shut and ran through the streets. As she sped past the village clock, she looked up and saw that it was half-past twelve, which meant the castle door had been locked for over an hour. She increased her speed — if she had to spend the night outside, it was better to do it at the castle rather than down in the village. If the sheriff saw her on the streets, he'd lock her in the dungeon for sure, or turn her over to the witch. Her chances were better with the night watchman who guarded the castle buildings and was known to be lenient. It shouldn't be hard to avoid him. She'd have to keep moving anyway to prevent herself from freezing to death. Already she could feel herself icing up, the water in her legs crystallizing.

By the time she had climbed the hill, the crystallization had spread from her legs, which were now pillars of ice, upward toward her heart. It was colder up here than it had been in the village. The wind was sharper, and puddles were scummed over with milky ice. It had started to snow, a slanting of white specks. She went over to the castle and looked up.

The perfume bottle was still there, but she couldn't reach it because the window was twelve feet above the ground. Looking for something to stand on, she walked behind the castle and in front of the laundry room window, where she found a plank frozen in the mud. Hoping it might open, she tried the window, but it was locked. Kicking the plank loose, she carried it to the wall beneath the bathroom window. It was then she heard footsteps coming along the front of the castle. The night watchman, she thought, and flattened herself against the wall. As the figure walked beneath the lamppost, she saw that it wasn't the night watchman but Don Quixote tilting along, hands in pockets, no doubt returning from Sancho Panza's. Wasn't that typical of him to appear when what she most needed right now was a real hero? Still, he was better than the night watchman.

She rushed out to meet him and looked into his startled eyes blinking against the snow. "Can you help me get in a window?" she said.

"What's the matter? Did what's-his-face leave you in the lurch?"

"He got into a fight and had to be taken to the hospital."

"Sounds like something he'd do," Don Quixote said. "You should have known better than to take up with that witless jock."

"Are you going to lecture me," Emily said, "or help me?"

Don Quixote shrugged. "I've helped other damsels in distress. Why not you? Just last week I got a girl in that bathroom window."

This was no doubt one of Don Quixote's fanciful delusions.

For someone who had done this before, Don Quixote certainly took his time. He sidled over to the wall, looked up at the window, walked back and forth in front of it several times before making an attempt. And then, when he finally got a grip on her waist to boost her up, it was too late.

There was the crunching of iced puddles; the night watchman was coming.

"Quick!" Don Quixote said, "put your arms around me."

Emily was too taken aback to refuse.

"If the night watchman sees us kissing, he'll leave us alone," Don Quixote said and started kissing her. He did this surprisingly well, in fact better than Walter. Maybe he *had* helped other maidens in distress. And he was right about the night watchman. When the old gentleman shone his flashlight on them and saw them kissing, he discreetly lowered the light and vanished. But, just to be on the safe side, they kept their lips together long enough for the snowflakes to make narrow drifts on their eyelids.

From a High Thin Wire

Finally Don Quixote said, "Well now, up you go."

It was a noisy operation. The window screeched loudly when Emily pushed it open. Her shoes scraped against the brick; her legs and feet were so numb she'd become clumsy. She kicked the perfume bottle to the floor. It rolled toward the door.

"Oh no," Emily groaned, "the witch will hear me."

Which is what happened.

By the time Emily had groped her way through the darkness, fumbled the bathroom door open and stepped into the corridor, the old crone was there waiting for her.

"So you made it at last." she croaked. Like Freud, the witch could see in the dark. She could see so well Emily felt she'd been stripped, that the witch's eyes saw through her winter coat, her skirt and sweater.

"Were you in the village?" the witch asked, not in her daytime voice but a voice that was hypnotically soft, a trick.

Emily was too cold and tired to lie.

"Yes," she said.

"Where in the village?"

"The rink."

"Ah, the hockey match. Was it exciting?"

"I didn't watch it that closely," Emily said.

"Why did you go then?"

Emily didn't reply.

"Was it so you could rendezvous with a young man?" the witch said craftily. "Or was it to see if you could get away with sneaking out?"

Emily refused to answer this one too.

"Well, now that you've tried it, I hope you're satisfied. You know the old saying about curiosity killing the cat. Oops, no offence, Freud," she cackled.

It was reassuring to hear her cackle, to know that she was her real self again. Perhaps now she would get on with pronouncing punishment. Would it be a month behind bars, a week cleaning toilets, a fortnight serving her afternoon brew?

But the witch again reverted to the unexpected. She switched on a flashlight and held it beneath her chin, transforming herself into an old woman, a tired old woman with wrinkles so deeply carved they seemed to go through skin to bone. She moved closer, and, for an awful moment, Emily thought she was going to touch her with one of those skeletal hands.

"I'm glad you got in safely," the witch half-whispered, as if they were in a conspiracy together. "When I checked your room and found it empty, I knew it was you who had left the bathroom window open, and I decided to wait up. I didn't want you to be left outside all night, which was what happened to me one winter's night when I was your age and stayed out with a young man. We nearly froze to death."

Imagine the witch trying to invoke an image of herself as a young woman locked out one winter's night with a young man. It was preposterous. If she believed this, the witch might even trick her into believing she'd had a lover once. But even as Emily tried to dismiss this invocation as sorcery, she couldn't help asking herself that if the witch *had* checked her room and found it empty, why hadn't she closed the bathroom window and shut her out for the night? That would have been the deserved treatment.

It was this doubt that started Emily thawing. She could feel her whole body melting; thin rivulets of water trickled down her legs, making small puddles at her feet. The thawing tired her, made her weak in the knees. She felt so weary that all she wanted to do was lie down and sleep. She wished the witch would sentence her so she could go to bed.

"What are you going to do with me?" she asked.

"Nothing, this time. I allow my girls to try it once. But of course if you were to try it again, which I hope won't happen," the witch said tiredly, "then I would have to punish you."

"Thanks," Emily said, though she was aware that thanking the witch was entirely out of bounds.

Then she broke another rule.

"Good night," she said.

The hockey game put Irene in the hospital for a week; the doctor suspected a concussion. After Irene got back to the residence, Emily bumped into her in the corridor one day. She told Irene that the witch had caught her climbing in the window after the hockey game. In fact, she even suggested the old girl had put out a hand and helped her up; Emily almost believed this herself. After delivering this punch line, she waited expectantly for Irene's disapproval, but Irene seemed not to have heard. She was busy showing Emily the diamond Walter had given her; they were being married at Easter. Emily didn't bother telling Irene that she had jumped into the moat.

Emily had leapt with stunning visual effect, hair streaming behind her, arms outstretched for that final flight, before landing with a satisfying splat. Once she was down, Emily realized the water was not at all as she had imagined. The curdle of bobbing heads was merely a protective crust; beneath it, the moat was clear and green, and, as Don Quixote had said, the water was warm. Though he claimed the whole thing was a mirage, he dove in from time to time. To keep her company, he said.

Passage by Water

Emily didn't see the face of the night nurse, though the same woman came into her hospital room three nights in a row and shone a flashlight at her. The round blinding arc swept through the dark, across the metal bed, a searchlight tracking a lone prisoner in a night compound.

The first time the night nurse came into her room, Emily was hallucinating. Ten days before, she'd had a bladder repair, an operation necessitated by child-bearing. Before the operation, it had flopped down loosely, shapeless as a collapsed balloon, which meant she spilled urine whenever she jumped, ran or sneezed. Now her bladder was sewn to her pubic bone, so tightly stitched into place that it felt like an old leather shoe that has become wet, then left to dry stiff and hard in the sun. Its muscles had stopped working. Here she was, a thirty-seven-year-old housewife unable to pass water. She wanted to disown her body. She felt foolish, helpless, as if she were inhabiting a baby's body. Except that any baby was born being able to do what she couldn't. Babies came into the world screaming their anger and wetting themselves freely. Emily could do neither.

Before Emily had gone to sleep, Mrs. Schoenburg, the afternoon nurse, a soft-spoken, motherly woman, had brought Emily new painkillers, two round, green pills. She took the pills eagerly. Her stitches hurt, and the tube the doctor had inserted through her stomach wall into her bladder was uncomfortable. The tube had a miniature white plastic tap on it as tiny as one on a dollhouse sink. The other end was connected to a plastic canteen, a Uripac, into which her bladder emptied.

Mrs. Schoenburg emptied the afternoon's urine into the stainless steel kidney pan, poured it into a pitcher, then wrote 800 cc on the record sheet. "That's only 800 cc for the day." She frowned.

"But I drank five cups of tea, four glasses of juice and two cups of coffee, and it was emptied this morning!"

"Ah well. Never mind," Mrs. Schoenburg consoled her. "Perhaps the morning nurse forgot to put down her entry." She checked the record sheet. "Yes, that's right. There's nothing down for this morning. That accounts for it."

Mrs. Schoenburg reached over and switched off the light.

"Do you think I'll be able to go tomorrow?" Emily's voice was wistful.

Mrs. Schoenburg patted her arm comfortingly. "It's early yet. Usually it takes a week or two to get along. Every woman's different. Some women are tricklers, going a little more each day until they're back to normal. Other women are gushers; they just pass water all of a sudden. My guess is you'll be that kind, though it's hard to say. The important think is to push fluids and relax. That's the secret. Now you get some sleep."

Emily's hallucination began with the night light, an orange cube recessed into the wall at the foot of her bed. When she came out of sleep, her eyes focussed on the orange cube glowing queerly in the dark. Emily blinked. The orange light sparked, flickered, became two. Emily closed her eyes. She heard a rush of whirling air near the door. She blinked again and saw something dark by the wall, something that whirled and spun like a top, an elongated top, a column, a pillar of black, mummy-bandaged. As it whirled closer, the bandages unwrapped themselves, lengthening, snapping off ceilings and walls. The mummy whirled around the foot of the bed, then veered toward the window, spinning. Suddenly it tilted itself and came straight toward Emily; there was no mistaking its intent to attack her. Its orange eyes narrowed to glowing slits, its black bandages flapped across her feet, her legs, her chest then up to her face, slapping at her nose, her mouth, smothering her. Emily's hands went up to tear them away. She opened her mouth to scream, to protest, to breathe, but no sound came out.

The white arc of light swept across the bed, incurious, routine. Emily sat up in its glare shaking her head to free herself, pawing the air. Her chest was heaving, sweat was running down her back. Then strips of black snaked around her arms.

"A bad dream?" the night nurse asked from the doorway. Her voice was hollow like it was coming through a long metal tube.

"Not a bad dream. It was worse than that. It was a hallucination," Emily said slowly. "It was terrifying."

The night nurse didn't ask for details but kept the flashlight trained on Emily's face. All Emily could see of her was a low, stocky shape blocking the doorway.

"It must have been the green pills," Emily went on. "They must have caused it."

Still the night nurse stayed where she was, one of her hands holding the door open, the other the flashlight.

Emily wanted to shout, "Get that light off my face!" But she couldn't say it, just as she'd been unable to scream.

"I'll make a note of it on your chart," the night nurse said and, snapping off the flashlight, went out the door, leaving it ajar.

A corridor of yellow light, shining water, open sunny fields shone bright and warm beyond the door. Emily kept her eyes on the warm light, listening for sounds; the ringing phone, tapping oxfords, murmuring voices from the nursing station across from her room. Finally, as she was sliding into sleep, gently this time, a narrow letter being eased into a wide envelope, she heard a voice. It seemed to be coming from a valley far away past the fields and shining water.

"Miss-us," the voice called, plaintive, needing rescue. "Miss-us."

It was the old Italian lady two doors away in 310, six weeks in hospital with a gall bladder operation. Emily heard her every night calling the nurses; she never used the buzzer. Sometimes she called for an hour before the night nurse finally went to her.

In the morning, Emily drank a glass of juice, a glass of milk and two cups of coffee from her breakfast tray. After she had bathed and powdered herself, she pinned the offensive Uripac to the inside of her nightgown, where it didn't show except as an unnatural bulge on her hip. She imagined she resembled a diseased tree whose trunk was distended, the sort she saw in front of people's houses, varnished and hung with signs and lamps. Emily thought they made obscene use of a deformity.

She went into the corridor, crossed to the kitchenette, opened the fridge and forced down two glasses of apple juice. Then she began to walk. Down one side of the wing, past bare walls painted buttercup yellow, across the end of the corridor where the colour changed to turquoise, then along the other wing where the walls were bubble-gum pink. The colours were so determinedly cheerful, so garishly bright; they looked as if they had been chosen from a package of Easter egg dye. Although the floors were unblemished by scuffs or stains, a uniformed man was buffing the shining tiles with an electric polisher. He kept his head down, avoiding the string of women trailing past. One woman, a day out of a hysterectomy, staggered past, pale, unsteady, holding onto her metal intravenous stand for support. Clear fluid dripped down a tube into her arm; she looked like a prisoner of war surrendering to some ingenious method of water torture. Other women, three or four days out of surgery, walked gingerly, one hand on the corridor railings, the other holding their stomachs. Some women managed to do this unobtrusively, as if they were merely intent on keeping a hand pocketed; others were more careless, beyond modesty, boldly pushing hands against their incisions.

Though her stitches pulled, Emily walked straight, hands at her sides. She walked and walked, stopping at the end of the corridor where there was a large picture window. Sealed behind the glass, she heard no outside noises, saw no sign of movement except smoke from chimneys curling upward toward the low forehead of winter sky. The city was locked in white Siberian silence, in square straight bars of concrete, plate glass and pavement. Emily kept walking until she thought the morning fluids had worked themselves into her bladder, and she felt the urge to have a bowel movement. That was important, Mrs. Schoenburg had said, some women went by doing the two together.

Emily was sitting on the toilet with a magazine propped up on top of the disposal can, reading, trying to keep her mind off going. The tap was carefully adjusted to simulate a gentle flow of water, a small brook falling over stones. In Emily's lap was a basin of warm water in which she held her hands. She couldn't figure out why keeping her hands in warm water should induce the urge to urinate, but it did. She felt her bladder muscles pull in slightly. But the sensation was so weak that it had no effect. She tried to relax by forming a mental picture of herself as a sleek jet flying at cruising speed, moving effortlessly through the air, coming in for a landing, coasting onto the runway, stopping, opening up the baggage compartment, the suitcases dropping out, one by one.

She had a bowel movement, but no urine came with it. The bathroom had a rich, fecund smell that was comforting. At home, she used Pine Fresh to get rid of the odour, but since being in the hospital, she'd grown more appreciative of the powerful smell of her own feces. She was reassured by it like a baby proudly filling its diapers.

The door burst open abruptly, almost knocking the basin of water off Emily's knees. A plump arm reached in, jerked up the disposal can lid, yanked out the white plastic liner and pulled the bag through the crack in the door. The magazine fell to the floor. Emily couldn't bend over to pick it up. There was no point anyway. The woman would be back again with a new plastic liner. There was also no point in resenting the intrusion. There were no secrets in this ward: cotton sacks containing sanitary napkins hung on doors, enema syringes and douches were thrown into wastebaskets for visitors to see, nurses and nurses' aides burst into the room without knocking, bringing in clean sheets, thermometers, catheters, medication, meal trays, water jugs. It was the same with the housekeepers. They started in the corridor at seven in the morning and kept coming into the room in erratic thrusts of energy: to dust, to mop, to clean the bathroom sink, disinfect the toilet bowl, empty the disposal can.

Both the housekeeper's arms and legs came into the bathroom this time as a new plastic bag was inserted into the disposal can. Emily recognized the plump limbs as belonging to Jessie. It was Jessie's voice she heard every morning outside her door first and loudest, grousing about the nurses and what they expected. It wasn't *her* job to pick up dirty laundry; it wasn't *her* job to carry out meal trays. Those nurses were always trying to get you to do work for them; you had to stand up to them, that's what you had to do.

Jessie disappeared again. Emily stood up, added more hot water to the basin, picked up the magazine, sat down and concentrated on choosing something to read. Most of the articles were about women who seemed freer than herself: "Do-It-Yourself-Divorces," "The Advantages of Being Bisexual," "Adoption for Singles," even the titles depressed her. She was so far behind the times; there seemed no hope of her catching up on even understanding what was going on.

The bathroom door was flung open again, and there was Jessie in full glory, her plumpness encased in a mint-green uniform, her frizzy hair framing puttyish skin. Jessie shoved the mop between Emily's legs. Or tried to. Emily resisted. The least the woman could do was ask her to move her feet.

Jessie poked the mop under the sink, whanging it roughly against the tiles. "You still on the can?" She grinned at Emily, showing a wide band of purplish gums above her dentures.

Emily nodded but kept her eyes on the magazine.

Jessie tilted her head to one side and leaned on the mop, bunching up her heavy breast. "Tried beer yet?"

Emily looked up. "Why? Is beer supposed to work?"

"Work! I'll say it works! Some of them younger doctors prescribe it. Maybe your doctor don't know about it."

"You can't have beer in the hospital."

"Ha! That's what you think. I know two women down in chronic keep wine in their closets. You can bet your bottom dollar their doctors know about it. There was a woman here last month in the same fix as you. She had beer." Jessie leaned over conspiratorially. "Kept it in her shower."

That would be a good place to keep it, Emily thought. She wasn't allowed showers, and the plastic curtain across the shower stall would conceal anything inside.

"See, what's good about beer," Jessie went on, "is it goes right through you so fast. Works like a charm."

"Maybe I should try it. I've tried everything else."

"That's the spirit. You get your hubby to bring you some beer next time he comes, and you'll pee all right." Jessie stabbed the corner with the mop, then closed the bathroom door, satisfied. Emily could hear her in the bedroom banging the mop against the baseboards, the closet door, the waste can.

Lena Whynaught was a big, bold girl who was Emily's seatmate in grade three at Sydney Mines Elementary, back when there were two to a desk. Lena lived in a shack on the outskirts of town with nine other kids and smelled stale, as if she ate, slept and played inside a breadbox. In November, Lena came to school with impetigo: yellow, oozing, crusted sores spotted her arms and legs. She was sent home and never came back. But before she left, she sat through one of Miss Frazee's lessons on manners. Halfway through the lesson, Lena put up her hand.

"Please, Miss. I got to pee."

Miss Frazee suspended the chalk over the blackboard, where she had been writing down different ways of answering the telephone. She smiled encouragingly. "That's not what we say, Lena."

Lena put a hand to her crotch. "Please, Miss. I got to piss."

The smile remained fixed. "What we say, Lena, is we have to go to the bathroom."

Even toilet wasn't good enough for Miss Frazee. An English teacher, Miss Frazee constantly exhorted them to refine their speech — the English language must not be corrupted with vulgarisms.

"But we have a privy, Miss!" Lena said, looking around the class, enjoying the audience.

Only then did the chalk touch the blackboard, the smile disappear. "All right, Lena. You may go. I'll see you after school."

The grade two teacher, Mrs. Fairweather, had made them hold up either one finger or two and say aloud number one or number two. Emily didn't know why it mattered for the whole class to know which you had to do until Squirt Layton told her. If you put up two fingers, Mrs. Fairweather didn't question how long you were gone from class, whereas you were allowed only five minutes for one finger. Most of the boys said number two until Mrs. Fairweather caught on and questioned them closely in front of everybody, threatening to write notes home to parents, making sure the big jobs, as she called them, were done at home.

The nurses called it passing water, the doctor voiding. Emily's husband, Don, said taking a leak and crap. When they were younger, her children said wee-wee and poop. Since then, Emily had taught them to say urinate and BM. Emily was no longer sure of these words. Choosing the right word had become important to her. She had the idea that, if she came upon a certain arrangement of words, it would have the power of a chant, and the muscles of her bladder would magically open like the doors of Ali Baba's cave. She remembered how effective school ground chants were in exorcising tattlers.

Tattle-tale, tattle-tale,
Tie you on the bull's tail.
When the bull begins to pee,
We will have a cup of tea.

Jody Strom was a little girl who used to play with Emily's ten-year-old daughter, Megan. Until Emily caught her with her pants down defecating under the spruce tree on the front lawn. When Emily asked her what she thought she was doing, Jody simply pulled up her pants and walked home, leaving Emily staring down at droppings lined up like a row of sausages in front of the tree. No dog would do that. The child must want attention. She'd better tell Marg Strom. Since the divorce, Marg had gone back to university to study social work. She was away all day. Jody must be trying to tell her mother something.

Emily waited until she thought Jody would be in bed, before crossing the street. Through the window, she could see books and papers spread over the kitchen table. Marg came to the door wearing reading glasses.

Emily tried to be brief. "I hate to bother you, Marg, but I think you should know that Jody's been defecating on our front lawn. Judging from the number of droppings, it looks like she's been doing it for a couple of weeks." Emily felt this was a reasonable beginning: a statement of fact.

But Marg was annoyed. "Come off it, Em. Did you come all the way over here to tell me about a few turds? I've got a term paper due tomorrow."

"Well, if it was *my* daughter doing it, *I'd* want to be told." Emily didn't know why she felt it necessary to explain this.

"You and I are different. I don't let details like that bother me. I've got better things to do with my time."

Emily wasn't about to let this pass. "Perhaps you'd better spend more time with your daughter instead of at the university. I mean it is social work you're taking, isn't it? What better place to start than at home!" The words flew out of Emily's mouth like tongues of fire. "Maybe you should take the time to see what your daughter's done to our lawn. And when you come, bring a shovel!"

After she had stormed home, Emily felt terrible to have said so much, or to have said it the wrong way. There were two other children besides Jody and it must be hard raising them alone. The next morning, she went to the florist and bought a white rose in a bud vase, getting Megan to take it over, to show Marg she was sorry. Marg never acknowledged it, which Emily took as further proof of her failure to speak her mind without going too far.

It had reached the point where she would avoid making a complaint even when it was justified. She did this with her family; day after day she picked up dirty clothes, wet towels, newspapers, wiped up spilled milk and mud tracked as far as bedrooms, saying nothing. There was no one around to say anything to anyway, they were all off to work or school when she set to cleaning up, muttering, shaking her head. Then one day she would burst open angrily; the whole family — Don, Tom, Megan, Jimmy — came under fire. She overstated her case, played the martyr, exaggerated the wrongs until she became disgusted by her dramatization, her inability to be casual and matter-of-fact.

"Maybe you should go back to teaching," Don said to her after one of these sessions. "I don't think you're cut out to stay home."

Contrite, determined to reform, to become the all-giving earth mother, Emily would scrape off Don's windshield, start his car for him, pick up the children's clothes, take out the garbage, begin the cycle all over again.

Emily had been drinking beer for two days, averaging three bottles a day. She had one after her nap, taking the bottle with her into the sitz bath. She ran two inches of water as hot as she could stand and sat in it drinking beer. The idea, according to the nurses, was to pass water in the water. To Emily, this was tantamount to going in the sea. She tried to recall those lazy summer days as a child when she lay like a fish in a tidal pool at Ingonish. She leaned back in the bath, closed her eyes, the beer making her light-headed, and tried to hypnotize herself into thinking she was a fish that rested in the shallows, the fluids of its body moving with the tide. It didn't work.

She had another beer with Don during evening visiting hours. After he had left, she tried to squeeze in another. It was really too much. One night, a Saturday after Don had gone home early to watch the hockey game, Emily took a bottle of beer with her into Gina's room. She had taken to visiting the old lady in the evening, thinking that if she got more attention, she'd be less likely to call out during the night. Whenever she visited Gina, Emily took something with her: a flower, a chocolate bar, a magazine.

The first time Emily went into Gina's room, she'd been appalled by its starkness. When she walked past other rooms, she saw bouquets of flowers lined up on window sills: roses, mums, carnations done up with ferns and bows. There were boxes of chocolates, books, magazines and always a new pastel-coloured bathrobe folded across the foot of the bed. The old lady had nothing. Except for the empty water glass on the night table and the woman herself sitting in the corner chair with a blanket over her knees to cover up what the blue hospital gown did not, the room might have been unoccupied. Gina had the abundant white hair and sad, brown eyes of a defeated matriarch. Even the sagging, tea-coloured jowls couldn't disguise the strong cheekbones, the thrusting jaw. There was no smile whenever Emily entered the room, only a nodded acknowledgement that another brief distraction had come her way, like the feather of a migrating bird fluttering into her lap.

Tonight when she came into the room, Emily asked the old lady if she would help her out by drinking some of her beer.

"I like wine, Missus," Gina said. "But I take beer."

Emily poured a glass full of beer and handed it to the old lady, who took it with a firm hand. "How's it going tonight?" Emily said.

"Terrible. The doctor says I go home tomorrow."

"Why, that's wonderful."

Gina took a swallow of beer and eyed Emily balefully. "Maybe for you. Not for me. My husband have bad heart. He can't help me to bathroom. My son works."

"Isn't there someone who could help you, a VON nurse?"

"Maybe. I like to get a woman in but my son won't pay. He wants me to cook for him. I'm too old to do the work. He should get a wife. He stay with us because he wants the house my husband and him build a long time ago. When my husband die, my son put me in place for old people." Gina shook her head. "In Italy, my mother turn over in grave."

Despite, or maybe because of, Gina's pessimism, Emily couldn't resist the urge to patronize. "I'm sure once you get home that things will work out for the best."

"Maybe, Missus," Gina said sourly, "maybe." She finished the beer and held the empty glass up for Emily. Emily took the glass to the bathroom, rinsed it out and brought it back three-quarters full of water. The old woman waved it away.

"Is there anything I can do for you before I go?"

"No, Missus. No." Gina said. "Nothing."

Her sad eyes dropped to her lap. Emily's visit was no more, no less than she'd expected.

Emily had been in bed an hour staring into the dark. As usual, her door had been left ajar. But the corridor of yellow light no longer shone bright and warm beyond her door. She could hear a storm of laughter and word gusts coming from the nursing station. She remembered it was Saturday and thought the nurses must be having a party. She got up, unpinned her Uripac from the bed and padded across the bare floor to the door.

"Missus! Missus! I need you!" With all the commotion in the nursing station, Gina's plaintive voice might have been coming from the bottom of an abandoned well. "Missus! Come quick! I need you."

Obviously no one was going to help the old lady, and putting on her slippers, Emily padded down to 310. When she pushed open the door, Gina whined, "Oh Missus, you came. I got to go bad," and, assuming Emily was the night nurse, said, "That lady, she gave me beer."

"I'm not the nurse. I can't take you," Emily said, "I'll ring for someone." She went over to the bed and pushed the buzzer.

The old woman grabbed hold of Emily's arm. Emily tried to pull away, but the grip tightened as Gina began to lever herself up with Emily's arm.

"Please Missus. You take me. That night nurse mean. She won't come. She hates me."

Emily jerked away. "No! I can't lift you or I'll pull my stitches. I'll go up to the desk and get you a nurse."

When she stood squarely in front of the nursing station, simply stood there until the laughter subsided and they noticed her, she was aware how strange she must look, at least to herself if not to them. They were used to women whose nightgowns were hitched up by plastic tubes exposing white legs and shaved pubic hair. One of the nurses came forward, and Emily knew by the stocky shape of her that she was the night nurse. She was unprepared for the youngness of the face, the childish snub nose, the wide flatness of the eyes. She didn't look mean or hateful, only untouched by experience.

"The old lady in 310 needs to go to the toilet," Emily told her.

"She's always saying that," the night nurse said. "When we get her up, she doesn't go. Later she wets the bed."

"I'm sure that happens," Emily conceded, "but the fact is she definitely has to go now."

She didn't stop there. She knew she might think she was interfering, but she didn't care. She was going to say it anyway. She looked at the night nurse. "You know," she said, "it wouldn't hurt to remind yourself that you might be eighty-four someday and needing attention."

Then she stomped across the hall, got into bed and went to sleep.

Two hours later, her bladder woke her up. The sensation to go was so strong she got up too quickly and was pulled back by the tube pinned to the bed. She bumped into the night table. It banged against the wall. Fumbling with the pin, she tried to free herself, but she couldn't manage it and she yanked out the tube, disconnecting the Uripac from her bladder. Not bothering to turn on the light, she followed the well-worn path to the bathroom. As she was settling onto the toilet, she kicked over an empty beer bottle she'd forgotten to put back in the shower. It clattered into the corner.

The night nurse opened the bathroom door and shone the flashlight on Emily's face. "I heard banging. Are you all right?"

"Of course I'm all right," Emily said. "And don't shine that flashlight in my face."

The flashlight beam swung to the floor and circled the bottle. "It looks like you've been drinking," the night nurse said.

"That's right," Emily said triumphantly. "And I'm peeing too."

"You're what?"

"I'm PEEING!" Emily shouted it out. *Open Sesame.* The proud rush of yellow fluid came warm between her legs.

Mrs. Schoenburg had been bang on: she was a gusher all right.

The Tail of the Female

I t's an ill-defined, late winter day. Earlier in the week, sun has melted snow into small deserted islands that now look like shards of ice floes stranded on a shambled beach — last year's grass. Leafless trees seem without protection against the grey cold. The weight of the cold presses against the inside of the house.

Fergie and I are sitting at my kitchen table Thursday noon, eating shrimp sandwiches and drinking white wine. We are talking about George Menzies, a kid in my English class who's been acting up lately. Bald-headed and big-eared, Fergie is one of these tall men with soft bellies, thin legs, big feet. He is affable, paternalistic, used to taking charge. He has the reputation for being a no-nonsense principal. True to form, he's telling me not to worry, he'll handle Menzies. Right after lunch, he'll boot him out of school for a week; that'll make the kid stop and think.

With one large hand scissoring the stem of his wine glass, Fergie's rotating the stem around his grey flannelled knee as he talks. The other hand is rubbing the pregnable underside of my arm where it lies exposed white on the table. I make no effort to move my arm, to say maybe I should handle George Menzies myself. I simply sit there feeling the coolness of his finger against my warm arm.

We are still dressed when my ten-year-old daughter, Rachael, who usually eats lunch at school, storms in the back door and heads for her bedroom, not even a nod toward Fergie.

"I'm sick," she says.

I get up, follow her down the hall. She flops on her bed, draws her knees up to her chest.

"Do you want lunch, soup maybe? Ice cream?" I ask her.

"I'm not hungry," she says and closes her eyes, sighing dramatically.

Rachael is an actress. Sometimes I wonder if it's a talent bestowed on the youngest to gain attention or whether it's a survival skill; she's the only girl in the family, at the end of three boys. Every time fifteen-year-old Drew, the only brother still living at home, bullies her, she's being assaulted, murdered, burned alive. Removal of a splinter brings shrieks and tearful pleadings. Failing a spelling test can precipitate the flu. With Rachael, the diagnosis is seldom straightforward.

I put my hand on her forehead. It's hot. Fergie comes into the room and pats her clumsily on the shoulder. She doesn't react. No smile. Nothing. Usually she hugs and kisses him. This, more than anything else, tells me she's sick. Still, I'm casual. I have never babied my daughter; girls grow up to be child-bearers, some divorcees like myself.

"I think maybe I'd better have the doctor look at you. Can you walk?"

Rachael nods, sits up, eases herself off the bed and, holding her stomach, limps out of the room.

At the front door, she turns to me and bursts into tears. "I want Raggedy Ann," she sobs.

"I don't know where she is," I tell her, which is only partly true; now that I know there's something seriously wrong, I want to get on with it.

"She's in the basement in the doll box," Rachael says and cries harder.

While Fergie carries her out to the car, I go downstairs and rummage through boxes I never got around to unpacking; most of them contain twenty-two-year-old wedding presents, mostly silverware, now my hedge against inflation. Since the divorce two years ago, Rachael has kept her dolls in the basement. It's as if she's wanted to maroon them there along with the tarnished silverware. Finally I find the right box and pull out the doll. Then I go outside and hand the doll to Rachael, whom Fergie has bundled into the back of my car.

Fergie goes back to school and I drive Rachael to the clinic. We spend the afternoon sitting on plastic chairs in the doctor's waiting room. In between, there is an examination, a blood test, another examination. The doctor, Esther Nemetz, tells me she's not sure if it's a severe case of gastritis or appendicitis. She's called a surgeon friend of hers to come in for a second opinion. We wait another hour, sitting side by side in the waiting room, Rachael's head on my lap. At five, Dr. Entwhistle, the surgeon, arrives and orders Rachael to the hospital for an operation I once had myself, an emergency appendectomy.

At the hospital, Rachael is admitted, X-rayed, then taken upstairs to her room. I hold Raggedy Ann and watch while the nurse helps my daughter undress. Rachael climbs into bed and the nurse unscrews her earrings, two gold stars, and hands them to me. In the hospital's bleached light, Raggedy Ann stands out as the one who is loyal and patriotic. This has nothing to do with her red and white striped leggings, red hair, white apron. It has to do with a dependable domesticity; her country is the kitchen. She carries with her the picture of a pioneer hearth, soup bubbling in a cast-iron pot, cradle by the fire.

The nurse gives Rachael a hypo.

Two orderlies come into the room and wheel her bed down the corridor toward the operating room. The younger of the two notices Raggedy Ann. "What's your dolly's name?" he says.

By now, Rachael is feeling better, the hypo is beginning to

take effect, she's getting a lot of attention. I wonder if she will tell the orderly what a stupid question he's asked; she seldom overlooks one. The orderly seems absurdly young to me, his brownish beard barely begins to fuzz his flushed cheeks, but he has a tousled poignance that isn't lost on Rachael. She decides to play a game.

She holds up Raggedy Ann. "Would you like to kiss her?" she says, fluttering her eyelashes. Rachael has green eyes, long lashes. She's going to be a real beauty, Fergie says.

"I'd rather kiss *you*," the orderly says and tweaks her toe. Then he turns away, negotiating the bed around the corner. The game's over.

But Rachael holds him to it. "Well, come on then," she challenges him, smiling, her teeth even, white, none of them missing; my daughter has never gone through an awkward stage.

While the other orderly, a fat middle-aged man, grins good-naturedly, the young orderly stops wheeling the bed and bends over to plant a dutiful kiss on my daughter's cheek. At the last moment, Rachael deflects her head, and the kiss lands on her mouth. There's a movement beneath the white sheet. Slowly, seductively, she's rubbing her toes together.

Down on the operating room floor, I am allowed as far as the desk. There, a nurse comes and wheels Rachael away. Before she leaves, I give her a kiss on the forehead.

"See you later, Mum," Rachael says, dismissing me. Not for a moment does she look for help in my face. Instead, she begins to talk to the nurse.

I find a pay phone near the cafeteria and call Rachael's father, Gary. He offers to take the night shift. He doesn't mention bringing Frances, which is just as well. Rachael knows it's Frances, not I, who is her rival.

Then I phone Fergie.

"How is she?" he says.

"Fine. Flirting with everyone in sight."

He laughs. Fergie, who has grown sons only, is amused by Rachael's precocity, but it disturbs me. It's as if she's trying to make up for what she doesn't have, which is two parents living together. By the time Rachael was born, Gary was wedded to his consulting business, I to our sons. Gary saw this first and hired Frances, who eventually became his lover.

I want to tell Rachael she's looking in a precarious place for love, or at least a precarious place for one so young. I want to tell her that I too have looked in precarious places. To warn her that my relationship with Fergie probably won't last, that I need something more than a lover, which is to stand on my own two feet.

"At least it takes her mind off the operation," Fergie says.

"True enough."

"I'll get you a sub for the rest of the week," he says. "Call me after the operation's over."

The operation takes an hour. When they wheel Rachael out of the operating room and into the recovery room, Raggedy Ann is no longer in the crook of her arm but lying at the foot of her bed. Rachael has become the doll, her face plastic-moulded beneath synthetic brown curls, her lashes folded over pale, waxen cheeks. Rushing to her side, I listen for the reassuring sound of her breath.

I'm not supposed to be in the recovery room, and the nurse shoos me away. In the hallway, I meet Dr. Entwhistle. Dressed in hospital greens, he looks more like a workman than a surgeon.

"Your daughter's all right, Mrs. Fraser," he says. "We got the appendix out in plenty of time. The operation was routine except for one thing."

"What's that?"

"Her appendix was filled with pinworms."

"Pinworms. Where in the world would she get those?"

"Children often pick them up outside. They get into the anus from dirt piles, sandboxes, that sort of thing. They're very common. I'll rush a specimen through the lab to make certain. I must say I've never seen so many pinworms in a diseased appendix before. It was riddled with them."

"If pinworms are all that common, how come I managed to raise three sons without coming across them?"

Dr. Entwhistle shrugs. "Some kids get them, some don't. It's the luck of the draw." Then he goes on. "Your daughter's quite a charmer, isn't she? Not the least bit shy."

"She gave up playing in sandboxes when she was five," I tell him, but he doesn't get the connection because he goes on to say, "She could have picked them up just sitting in your own backyard."

When I get home, I look up "pinworm" in the dictionary.

PINWORM, Webster's says, *any of the small nematode worms that have the tail of the female prolonged into a sharp point and infest intestines of various vertebrates.*

My own appendix ruptured in the middle of the night. It was in Cape Breton, in spring, when ice floes were straggling down Cabot Strait. My father was away starting up a new business, and my older sister Jane, who had bronchial pneumonia, was allowed to sleep beside my mother in my parents' bed, a privilege never granted to me.

The sudden knifings woke me up, jolted me from sleep. I doubled up my legs, but this didn't help. I rolled on top of my knees and shoved their boniness into the pain, rocking, moaning. I didn't call out for my mother; I didn't know that the symptoms were unnatural — at thirteen I was without a record of pain. And my mother had told me how, after her mother had died, leaving her an orphan of nine, she had scrubbed floors for a foster parent until her knees bled, but she never cried. And my grandmother had fallen out of an apple tree when she was sixteen in Ireland and sustained a knee injury so severe she limped badly the rest of her life, but she never complained.

By morning, the pain had gone but my legs were stretched out straight, there was no feeling in them. Eventually my mother came into my room. But only after she had carried a breakfast tray upstairs to my sister. She said she was surprised to see me still in bed, why didn't I get up? When I didn't answer, she gave me a quick glance, then a look of sudden confusion.

My mother's face was a road map, and only by looking at it could I get my bearings. This time I was lost and could no longer see the white ice floes in the blue harbour. I was in another country, a tropical forest where everything was green. A leafy hand brushed my forehead. Rain dripped onto my cheeks. An exotic bird shrilled like a telephone. Two men carried me away on a stretcher. I remem-ber my sister was there, standing in her nightgown near some steps, and my mother had the back of her hand pressed to her open mouth.

I was taken far away to a place flooded with light so blinding I had to close my eyes against it. When I woke up, it was night again, and I was in a tent somewhere in the tropical forest, convinced that I had been tortured. My skin was on fire, my belly hurt, and my mouth was a crusted wound of thirst. I opened my mouth to scream, and a wild pig squeal came out. I was answered by a movement outside the tent. There was a loud trumpeting call. Footsteps. I opened my eyes and saw a pale moon circle through my tent wall.

Then a voice parrot-sharp. "What is it, Mrs. Dubinsky?"

"The pain," the voice gouged out of her. "Something for the pain."

"Right here. I have it. Turn over, Mrs. Dubinsky. Turn over."

A groan, a movement, a heaving elephant of pain.

"That's right."

A grunt, a thrust.

"That's it. There you are"

A guttural moan going on and on.

"You'll have to be quieter, Mrs. Dubinsky. We don't want to waken the others. Shh! The girl next to you has just come through an emergency operation. Quiet now."

The moon circle vanished.

By the time the sun came up, I was back in my own country, but my mother was nowhere in sight. I heard a breakfast trolley rattling over the tiled floor. The white curtain around my bed swayed imperceptibly from the movement of trays being carried back and forth. None came for me.

The woman with the pain hadn't stirred.

"Mrs. Dubinsky had a hard night of it," I heard a fat voice say. It was coming from across the room. "Yes, Dearie, I'll have tea, thank you. The coffee makes me sick at my stomach. . . . Woke me up she did. The pain was something awful. Poor soul."

From somewhere down the row of beds, I heard a thin, tremulous voice. "Cancer's the worst pain of all. It's a scourge. My brother went with it. Had a hole in his back you could put your fist into."

"Mrs. Dubinsky don't have it *there*, Dearie. She's got it all through her innards. Got to go through a tube even. It won't be long now."

A cup clattered in its saucer.

"Now ladies" — this was a narrow voice of a nurse — "let's talk about something more cheerful, shall we?"

My white curtain was pushed aside, and there stood the nurse bristling in white starch.

"How's the new patient this morning?" she said, and before I could answer, she had shoved a thermometer into my mouth and taken up my limp wrist. "The doctor will be here shortly."

The doctor was a weary, pale-looking man. While the nurse commanded his elbow with a tray of sterilized pads, tongs and a brown paper bag, he pulled back the covers and peeled off a wide swath of tape. Immediately, there arose the putrid odour of carrion flesh.

The odour came from my belly, my flesh, my body. One by one, the pus-soaked, foul-smelling pads were lifted off and put into the paper bag. I dared myself one quick look down there where it all was and saw my flesh trussed up like a raw turkey's with a tube sticking out of it. A tube. A long, white, rubbery tube draining out pus, greenish-brown.

From a High Thin Wire

My mother came to see me, bringing ginger ale. She didn't mention my sister's pneumonia. She closed the curtains around the bed, wrapping the two of us inside. I signalled her to come closer.

"You don't have to pretend," I whispered, "I know the truth."

"The truth about what?" my mother said.

"I'm going to die!"

My mother's forehead wrinkled into a network of tiny roads and tributaries. "Nonsense," she scoffed. "Where did you get such an idea?"

"The woman in the next bed to us is dying. She has cancer. She's got a tube in her just like me. They put me in here with her because we're both dying."

My mother had no answer for this. Her face collapsed into a thick, unreadable tangle and then went blank. It was as if she had been pushed over the edge of a cliff, and there was no way to break the fall.

Rachael is back in her bed. There's a square bandage on her arm where she's been hooked up to an intravenous tube. The bag of clear fluid hangs from a metal stand. There are three other beds in the room, but only one of them has an occupant. He's a year-old baby with his middle bandaged who is standing, holding onto the metal supports, crying for his mother.

Fergie has come with me to the hospital. In case Rachael needs him, he says.

A nurse comes in and takes the baby out into the corridor, walking him up and down to soothe him, but it's too late. Rachael is already awake. As soon as she sees me, she starts to cry. "My stomach hurts," she says.

"I know, Baby, I know." I stroke her forehead, which is hot.

"Where's Daddy?" she says, "I want Daddy."

"He'll be along soon."

"I want him *now*. Where is he?"

"He's probably held up in traffic," I tell her.

But Rachael won't be appeased. She begins to cry, large wracking sobs that must hurt her side. When I try to comfort her, she pushes me away. Then, abruptly, she stops crying and looks at me, cheeks flushed, eyes defiant.

"I want Fergie," she says.

Fergie, who has been standing discreetly aside, offers a riddle. He goes over, settles his long frame on the bed and takes her hand. "Did I ever tell you why the tomato blushed?" he says.

Rachael shakes her head no.

"It watched the salad dressing."

Rachael grins and wriggles her toes.

My father didn't come home after the operation; he kept in touch by phone. It was my mother who had me moved out of the ward for the terminally ill and into a private room. Once that was accomplished, she came to see me bearing a gift from my sister. It was a black silk bathrobe splashed with pink and orange flowers that had once belonged to my mother. As the elder sister, Jane thought herself its natural heir. Here she was giving it to me. If further proof of my impending death was needed, my sister had just given it to me.

"She would have brought it herself, but she's still running a temperature," my mother said.

"Is she sleeping in her own bed yet?" I had to know.

My mother didn't understand the importance of this question; jealousy was a luxury she couldn't afford. "As a matter of fact," she said, "she's still sleeping with me. I get more rest that way."

I saw the soft deterioration of flesh beneath her eyes, the blue deep as shadowed snow, but I kept on. I was relentless in the pursuit of my mother.

"At least she's not at death's door," I said. Then I asked her if she would bring me a rosary. We weren't Catholic. She brought me the Bible instead.

"You'll find lots of dramatic stories in there," she said.

I have never doubted the possibility that Rachael's sense of drama came from me. But now I see it as a physical manifestation, an appendage passed on at birth through generations of daughters; an invisible weapon, a sharp pointed thing we use to attack and, at the same time, defend.

The morning after Rachael's operation, I get into my car and drive to the hospital. It snowed during the night, a light powdering, enough to make causeways between the islands of old snow. This is temporary because the leaden ceiling has lifted, the large western sky is opening up; soon the sun will melt the slender white linkages.

The nurse at the desk tells me Rachael had a restless night. Gary left at two o'clock, but Rachael woke up twice after that. Though the nurse assures me she managed to calm her down, I am upset to hear this.

Since the divorce, Rachael has had trouble with Gary's promises. On Saturday, his visiting day, he'll phone her two or three times starting at nine. He can't make it until ten. At ten, he can't make it until eleven. It's sometimes noon before he comes for her. When I ask him why doesn't he come at nine and take her back to the apartment so she knows for sure, he says Frances wouldn't like it. What power Frances wields with her beauty. I have no memories of him trying so hard to please me, but perhaps they are there, packed away with the wedding presents. He takes Rachael to a movie, the zoo, the Planetarium. They go shopping and, guilt-ridden, he buys her clothes that are too adult for her, even lipstick, which I won't allow her to wear and which she's saving for grade seven dances. Already she tells me which boys in school are cute and which are weird. She and her friend Cynthia have made up a list of the cute ones. Once or twice, I've heard them phoning boys on the cute list. She and Cynthia like to put on the record player and dance in front of Rachael's bedroom mirror. Rachael puts on the hoop earrings she conned Gary into buying and swivels her hips like a belly dancer.

The baby in the bed across from her is gone, so Rachael sleeps on, her small face madonna pale, without artifice. Raggedy Ann's red mop of hair sticks out above the sheet.

At eleven, a nurse in a pink nylon pantsuit, a black bar on her chest with *Miss Barkhouse* lettered on it in white, strides into the room.

"Rachael," she says. "It's time to get up." Miss Barkhouse is young and confident.

Rachael opens her eyes, sees the nurse, then closes them again, as impervious to movement as a dozing turtle.

"Come on, Rachael," Miss Barkhouse says, "it's time for a walk."

"I don't want to walk," Rachael grumbles. "Leave me alone."

"Come now. That's no way to talk," Miss Barkhouse smiles encouragingly. "I'm here to help you."

"No." Rachael has dug in.

"Rachael," I warn her. Miss Barkhouse is being patient.

"No."

Miss Barkhouse switches her strategy, and pulling back the sheet, she says briskly, "I'm afraid you have no choice. You'll have to get up. Now."

"But my stomach hurts."

"Of course it does," Miss Barkhouse sympathizes. "But you can manage it. It'll be a short walk, just a few steps. Then you can get back into bed." She leans over, cranks up the bed. Taking hold of Rachael's shoulders, she says, "Mrs. Fraser, if you take her other shoulder, we can lift her into a sitting position."

As we slowly pull Rachael upwards, there is a sharp cry and Rachael sinks back onto the pillow.

"I can't," she sobs. "I can't."

And even I begin to wonder. "Isn't it a bit soon?" I say. "She was only operated on yesterday. Why don't we do it tomorrow?"

"Doctor's orders," Miss Barkhouse says. "It helps circulation. Speeds recovery."

So we try again. This time Miss Barkhouse eases Rachael's legs over the side of the bed first, and then we lift her into a sitting position. Miss Barkhouse pushes Rachael's feet onto the stool. When we pull her to her feet, she cries out sharply, but Miss Barkhouse keeps right on.

"Now slide one foot off the stool. Gently. That's it. Then the other. Good girl."

Rachael is sobbing now. Miss Barkhouse keeps urging her forward, talking to her, both of us supporting her, the intravenous stand wobbling behind. Rachael walks.

"I want Daddy," she cries with each step.

My hands dig deeper into her flesh. "He's not here. *I* am." I don't expect my words to register. Rachael has grown so used to my presence that I sometimes wonder if she thinks my life has been sifted through an egg timer stood end on end by others.

After Rachael has taken ten steps across the room, Miss Barkhouse says, "You can go back to bed now. You've gone further than most patients manage the first time up. Dr. Entwhistle will be pleased."

Rachael stops walking. "Why?" she says.

Miss Barkhouse blinks. "Why what?"

"Why will he be pleased?"

"Because he takes pride in his patients' recovery, that's why. It'll make him feel good to know that you're progressing quickly. Then he'll know he's done a good job."

"But *I'm* the one who's walking," Rachael says stubbornly.

"That's right," Miss Barkhouse says smoothly. "I don't know when I've seen a little girl walk as well as you do. But now it's time to get back into bed."

"No," Rachael says. "I want to go for a walk in the hall." And with surprising strength, she pushes both of us aside and grabs hold of the intravenous stand. "By myself."

Miss Barkhouse looks doubtful but she says nothing, merely follows Rachael's unsteady steps. I stand in the doorway, watching.

Rachael goes halfway down the corridor before she turns around and comes back. She's still walking when Dr. Entwhistle crosses the hall and sees her.

"Look at me," Rachael says, one hand on the intravenous stand, the other on her incision. "Aren't you proud of me?"

Dr. Entwhistle smiles. Without his operating greens, he looks boyishly handsome. "You bet I am," he says.

But then Rachael says, the rudeness in her voice unmistakable, "I don't mean you. I mean my mother."

For once, I don't correct her. "Of course I'm proud of you," I tell her. And give her a hug as she wobbles past.

"By the way," Dr. Entwhistle says. "I read your daughter's lab report this morning. It confirmed what I told you earlier. That her appendix was riddled with pinworms."

Rachael stumbles against the wall. She rights herself and keeps on going.

"You know," Dr. Entwhistle muses, "I find your daughter's case intriguing."

"Why is that?"

"The pinworms," he says. "Were they attracted to the appendix because it was diseased, or did the pinworms cause the disease? Which came first?"

But I pay no attention. Now that my daughter's out of the woods, that no longer is the question. Or if it is, the answer makes no difference.

Italian Spaghetti

"Brr, it's cold out there," Tom said. "I'd better light the fire." He came into the kitchen and set the scotch and the wine on the countertop. There were red dimes on his cheeks and frost at his temples. The frost made him look distinguished.

Leslie was standing at the sink hulling strawberries. "Not yet," she said, too sharply. "We only have those paper logs I made from newspapers. And what's left of the packing case."

The packing case was what their books had come in when they'd moved here to Toronto in the fall.

"It's okay. I brought in some wood scraps Old Man Proctor said we could use."

Old Man Proctor was their landlord. They lived in three rooms on the top floor of his rambling house. The apartment was drafty and gloomy, but Tom found it within easy walking distance of the university which meant Leslie could use their old Ford to get to her school out in Oakville. Leslie had fixed the place up with a sisal rug, boards and bricks, strategically placed plants. She didn't mind these frugal measures as long as they were temporary. She liked to think of her life in stages; right now she was in her scrimp-and-save stage. This attitude also helped in tolerating Old Man Proctor who, perhaps because the rent was low, seemed to think it within his rights to snoop in their apartment when she and Tom were out. Once Leslie came home early from school and found the diaphragm she had left drying on the bedroom window sill had been moved — this was when the pill had first come on the market and Leslie didn't want to risk the side effects, so she and Tom were putting up with the diaphragm instead. Another time she came home and found Old Man Proctor in their bathroom opening the medicine chest. He said he was checking for dry rot, and Leslie thought that was a strange place to look for it.

The old man had a teenaged granddaughter named Fay who thought she could sing. She came over late Saturday afternoons and endlessly practiced show tunes on his grand piano. Before Christmas, it had been songs from *Fiddler on the Roof*. Leslie didn't think she'd ever recover her fondness for "Sunrise, Sunset" since the granddaughter had strangled it. After Christmas, Fay moved on to *Showboat*. She had a small part in her school's spring production, Old Man Proctor proudly informed Tom when he'd gone down to pay the rent. The smallness of the part had not dampened Fay's enthusiasm for learning the entire musical score, which she sang off-key.

Fish gotta swim, birds gotta fly,
I'm gonna love one man till die.
Can't help lovin' that man of mine.

Every Saturday, her flat nasal voice travelled up the heat register to the third floor, seeking them out. She had not yet shown up this Saturday afternoon. Leslie was hoping Fay would get it over with earlier than usual today so their dinner guests wouldn't be subjected to the unwanted distraction, but so far she hadn't turned up. With any luck the girl had come down with laryngitis.

Leslie finished hulling strawberries and put them in the fridge.

The strawberries were a winter treat flown in from Florida or California. They were expensive, and Leslie was sure their dinner guests, Richard and Nancy, wouldn't be able to afford them. She had splurged on them to fancy up a cheap meal of spaghetti with meat sauce. Spaghetti was supposed to be popular with kids, or so she gathered from TV commercials, which she watched infrequently when she and Tom visited their parents in Nova Scotia. Nancy and Richard were bringing their kids, Paul and Charlotte. Leslie wasn't all that enthusiastic about the kids coming; by Friday afternoons she'd had enough of teaching garrulous school children and looked forward to weekends without kids. But Nancy had said there was no money in their budget for babysitters, and they had to bring them or stay home.

Leslie decided to make the most of it. She had brought coloured paper from school and made placemats — a rooster for Paul, a bunny for Charlotte — which she put on the card table in the kitchen. She had also made them a centrepiece of toothpicks and jelly beans and bought them each a colouring book and crayons to keep them occupied while the adults visited in the living room. For the adults, she had bought a red-checkered tablecloth to put on the kitchen table and dribbled wax over the sides of an empty wine bottle to create the Italian *ristorante* atmosphere.

"Tom, can you give me a hand with this table?" she said. "I want it in the living room."

Tom was sitting on the sofa, shoes off, reading the sports news, the weekend papers spread around him. "Sure," he said obligingly, and he set the paper aside.

It irked Leslie that he had gone right in and sat down without offering to help her first, that she always had to ask him to do things. With teaching and keeping up this place, she had more to do than she could manage. Didn't he notice that she never had time to sit down and read the newspaper?

Tom took one end of the kitchen table, Leslie the other, and they carried it into the living room.

"Careful," Leslie warned. She didn't want the tall candle she had stuck into the wine bottle to tip.

When the table was in place in front of the window, Tom said, "Anything else?"

Leslie looked at his rumpled trousers, the shirt-tail sticking out, the bare toes showing through his socks. He saw her frowning at his feet.

"Relax. I'll put on my shoes when the doorbell rings."

"Aren't you planning to change?" Leslie said.

"I hadn't planned on it. I showered this morning," Tom said. He sat down and picked up the sports page.

So Leslie put the chairs around the table. She tidied the wood scraps Tom had dropped in front of the fireplace. Then she picked up the loose newspaper sections and, folding them noisily, tucked them under the sofa.

"There!" she said.

Tom kept on reading.

Back in the kitchen ripping the lettuce, Leslie thought that Tom could afford to be casual about this dinner party because he'd never met Nancy and Richard. There was more at stake for her. Nancy and she had been roommates at university before Nancy had become pregnant with Paul and left in her third year to marry Richard. It was important to Leslie to renew this friendship, not only because she knew so few people in Toronto, but because, from the little she'd seen of Nancy since moving here, she perceived her as someone who needed friends, badly tied down as she was with two kids and with another one on the way.

From the living room, she heard the sound of Tom shuffling into his shoes. He came into the kitchen, put his arms around her waist and kissed her on the neck.

"Ummm," he murmured, "you taste good."

The doorbell rang and Leslie ducked under his arms and ran for the door.

Their four guests crowded into the tiny hallway, the kids behind their parents. Leslie and Nancy hugged each other. Leslie felt Nancy's swollen belly between them; in the month since she'd last seen her, Nancy had ballooned out. Richard kissed Leslie, his five o'clock shadow bristly against her cheek. Then he and Tom, who was watching all from the kitchen, shook hands formally. The children pushed past them into the living room and looked around.

"Where's the TV?" Paul said. He was dark and solemn like his father.

"Shame on you," Nancy scolded him. "You didn't come here to watch TV. Besides, you're not allowed to watch TV except on Sundays, and you know it's Saturday."

"What is there for me to do then?"

At five years of age, Leslie noticed, Paul had perfect enunciation, better than most of the first graders she taught.

"I have colouring books and crayons," Leslie said.

"We stopped at the library on our way here and got out new picture books," Nancy said. "All right, children, take off your coats and hang them up. Then you can look at these books. They're brand new. You'll be first to use them. Isn't that lucky?"

Charlotte took off her coat, but Paul made no effort to take off his.

"Get a move on, Paul," Richard said. "Remember what we told you on the subway. It's a privilege for you to be invited into the McIntosh's home. You can show your appreciation by behaving yourself."

Richard had a deep ministerial voice. It was his voice that had first attracted Nancy to him. She'd met him when he'd come to their campus with a debating team from a nearby university. She thought he had a sexy voice, she'd told Leslie in their room afterwards. This was true; Richard's voice was deep and compelling. Leslie could feel herself being pulled toward him, to a man physically huge, larger than life, not this short lean man with a narrow face, high forehead and small eyes.

At the time Nancy met Richard, he was studying for the ministry. When they were married, he told Nancy that although they were becoming man and wife, he would always love God first. Nancy accepted this as one of Richard's high principles, so she told Leslie, but the declaration weighed heavily on Leslie. It carried with it a sense of doom, a warning that, try as she might, Nancy would never get past being a handmaiden. Yet Leslie admired Richard; she admired a person with convictions, someone who was willing to take a stand, even if it was wrong. This was one thing that troubled her about Tom. He was so reasonable, so without an axe to grind, so willing to listen to someone else's point of view that Leslie sometimes wondered if he had one of his own. It didn't occur to her that his point of view might be an amalgam of other people's.

Paul had taken off his coat and dropped it on the living room floor.

"Pick it up," Richard said.

The boy obeyed. Leslie admired Richard for handling his son firmly. In school, she had children of permissive parents to cope with. Some of them refused to co-operate no matter how politely they were asked.

"Would they like to use our bed to read on?" Leslie said.

"Thanks, but I'd rather keep them here where I can watch them," Nancy said. Shepherding them toward the fire, she told them to sit on the floor and handed each child a book.

Paul took his book and headed for the bedroom.

Richard signalled him back. Paul dropped his knees to the floor, but he didn't look at the book. He stared moodily into the fire.

"Maybe they'd rather colour instead," Leslie said. She went into the kitchen and came back with the colouring books and crayons. She handed them to the children.

"What will you have to drink?" Tom said.

"A little wine," Nancy told him.

"Richard?"

"Scotch, if you have it."

This was a switch for him. When he was courting Nancy, he wouldn't touch liquor because his mother had been an alcoholic. Leslie supposed this sort of socializing went with selling insurance.

"So how's business?" Tom called from the kitchen.

Leslie was astonished Tom would bring up the subject of insurance. After they had been married a month, a bulky envelope arrived by registered mail. It was an investment portfolio Richard had made up for them even though he'd never met Tom. Tom had thrown it into the wastebasket. Here he was leaving himself wide open for questioning.

"Fine. Fine," Richard shouted back. "Record sales last year. By the way, did you ever get the portfolio I sent you? I tailored it especially for your needs. I do a lot of student portfolios."

Tom came into the room and handed Richard and Nancy their drinks.

"Yes, but we're not ready for that yet," he said easily. "Someday maybe, but not now." He went into the kitchen for the other drinks. When he returned, he said, "But you can tell me what you think I should look for in a few years from now." Tom sat on the sofa beside Richard and waited for him to take over the conversation. He was quite prepared to do this, to let someone else do all the talking.

"I lucked in on a tremendous sale," Leslie told Nancy. "A gift shop on Eglinton that's closing out. I found that red-checkered tablecloth half price." She waved toward her Italian table, then listed off the sale items in case there was something Nancy could afford. Since picking up their friendship, this was the sort of thing they talked about: fabric sales, food stamps, recipes for leftovers; they could go on for hours about domestic trivia. They took pleasure in talking about how they shamed store managers into giving generous refunds for stale bread and woody bananas. Nancy was more serious about this than Leslie, who regarded it as a bourgeois game that was fun as long as she didn't take it too seriously. But Nancy thought nothing of walking two miles to return a head of rusted lettuce. She dragged her kids all over Toronto tracking down bargains. Every penny saved went to pay off the loan from Richard's father, who was a lawyer. Richard had borrowed the money while he was in university, before he had found out about his father's mistress. Now that he had disowned his father, he couldn't pay back the money fast enough. He and Nancy still had no furniture but slept on the floor, sat on cushions and trunks. Their one luxury was the TV. Nancy managed these deprivations with proud defiance, a determined gaiety meant to ward off sympathy.

But Leslie felt sympathetic nonetheless. She was sure a dinner party, even a modest one like this, was a rare outing for her friend. Leslie sipped her wine and listened to Nancy. She was talking about a supermarket where she bought groceries by the case. While she explained the advantages and disadvantages of buying in bulk, Leslie saw Paul slip quietly out of the room and go into the bedroom, Charlotte following. Nancy didn't notice. She had moved on to a description of a course she was taking from the extension department on household money management. Since neither of them had much money to manage, Leslie could not sustain interest in the subject for long. She cast around in her mind to find some way of breaking new ground between them or at least reviving some of the old. She recalled the time she and Nancy had organized their Italy or Bust raffle. They had taken an art course together and were determined to go to Florence to see Michelangelo's *David*. Nancy had been so much fun in those days, willing to do anything on a dare. And you could always count on her; she was loyal. Leslie didn't think different lifestyles and husbands need interfere with old friendships; she still thought of marriage as a separate institution.

Charlotte came into the living room and announced she was hungry, so Leslie got up and went into the kitchen to boil water for the spaghetti. Nancy followed.

"What can I do to help?' she said.

"You can pour the kids' milk," Leslie said. "Or there's apple juice, if they'd prefer that. I set up this table especially for them."

"Why, you've made placemats and a centrepiece," Nancy said. "They'll be thrilled."

"Well, I wanted them to have a good time," Leslie said. "Us too."

"There's one thing I should mention. We like the children to eat with us. Would you mind if we moved the placemats into the living room?" Nancy said this so quietly, so easily, that it took Leslie a few moments to realize that she did mind.

From a High Thin Wire

But she was conscious of being the gracious hostess, so she put it obliquely. "You know the old saying: when in Rome, do as the Romans!" And she didn't move the placemats.

But Nancy persisted. "It's just that they might carry on if they're sitting separately. And, once you've established family policy on something, it's important to be consistent. When you have children, you'll understand what I mean."

When *I* have children, I won't drag them everywhere, Leslie said to herself. I won't foist them on other people. I won't let them take over my life. But she stalked into the living room to re-arrange the table.

"Let me help," Nancy said.

"No," Leslie said sharply, "you go sit down. You're here to enjoy yourself."

When Leslie pulled out the extra table leaf, she noticed that the new tablecloth was too short, the table edges showed at either end. She transferred the placemats to the ends to cover up this discrepancy and put the jelly bean centrepiece beside the waxed wine bottle. So much for atmosphere. But then the incongruities of the table setting struck her as comical and she snickered — at them and her own pettiness. She lit the candle.

She looked at Tom and said, "Could you pour the wine?"

She thought he looked relieved to be asked.

Richard took the children into the bathroom to wash; Paul had black crayon on his hands.

After they were seated, the couples opposite each other, the children at either end, Tom poured the wine. The salad and bread were passed. Leslie got up and handed round the plates of spaghetti and meat sauce. While they ate, Richard regaled them with a story about last summer's vacation, which they spent in a pup tent in the pouring rain. As a child, he said, his parents had always taken him to expensive hotels for holidays and dumped him with a babysitter, so he thought of camping as a novelty. Richard had a talent for description; it was he who wrote cheerful descriptions of the year's activities in a mimeographed newsletter as if he was determined to assuage the unhappy Christmases of his childhood.

"Can we go camping next year?" Charlotte asked, her words squashed in with the spaghetti.

"Don't talk with your mouth full," Nancy said.

Charlotte swallowed obediently. She was a co-operative child, blond and sturdy like her mother.

Nancy turned to help Paul, who had eaten a piece of bread and was sitting with his hands in his lap, his spaghetti untouched.

"You'd better start eating or you'll get behind," Nancy said.

"I can't eat this," Paul complained. "It falls off my fork."

"Certainly you can. All you have to do is use your fork and spoon together." Nancy picked up his fork and spoon and put one in each of his hands. Then using her hands to guide his, she said, "You take your fork and hold it against the spoon, then wind the spaghetti around it like this, see? Isn't that easy?" she popped the spaghetti into his mouth. "That's the way they do it in Italy!"

"Why doesn't he cut it with a knife?" Leslie said. She had seen Charlotte cut hers. "It does slide of the fork."

"Nonsense," Nancy scoffed. "He hasn't even tried it yet."

Paul made a half-hearted attempt at twisting the spaghetti around the fork, holding it jerkily against the spoon, but, when he failed, he dropped both utensils onto the plate, sat back and stared at his lap. Nancy had dressed him in a suit, probably a cast-off of Richard's made over. He looked like a sullen old man.

"Did Tom tell you he changed his thesis topic?" Leslie said. "Tell them, Tom."

Her husband had eaten his spaghetti but had left his wine. He was leaning forward, elbows on the table, eyes averted, far away. He did this sometimes when the going got rough, retreated to some lonely place, a northern wilderness where no one could follow. Don't go, Leslie said to herself, don't go. And Tom came back.

"With the necessity for better ecology escalating every day," he said, "I decided to concentrate on environmental engineering." He went on expanding, explaining. Richard asked good questions and together they took up fifteen minutes. During this time everyone had finished their spaghetti except Paul, who still stared into his lap.

"Eat your spaghetti," Richard said.

"I can't." Paul poked a strand of spaghetti into his mouth with a finger then sucked it inward with a satisfying slurp.

"That's enough," Richard said. "Eat it properly, the way your mother showed you."

"Why don't I take some off his plate?" Leslie suggested. She felt she should do something to make up for the mistake of serving spaghetti. If she'd known it was going to be this much trouble, she'd have settled for hot dogs. "I probably gave him too much," she said and reached for his plate.

Richard put out a restraining hand. "No," he said. "He'll eat it. He's just being stubborn."

Leslie looked at Tom, but he'd retreated again. She was angry at him, at Richard and Paul. It was clear father and son were locked in a stalemate. What were the rest of them supposed to do while this silly game was being played out? Sit and wait for the kid to eat? Well, she wouldn't. She got up and carried the plates into the kitchen.

Nancy gave Charlotte a jelly bean from the centrepiece, then she turned to Paul. "When you finish your spaghetti, you can have some of these candies for dessert," she said.

Leslie bristled. Wasn't that ridiculous? Once a kid dug himself into a hole as deep as Paul's, it took more than bribery to get him out. You didn't need kids of your own to figure that out. She spooned out limp strawberries, added cream and passed them around. They were eaten in silence. The candle burned low. The fire went out. Leslie brought in coffee.

Tom stood up. "I'm taking my coffee to a more comfortable chair. Anyone care to join me?" He looked at his wife.

Leslie left the table. Then Nancy and Charlotte got up. Leslie noticed Nancy's hand shaking when she picked up her cup. Coffee spilled onto her maternity dress, no doubt one she had made especially for tonight. Why didn't Nancy say something to Richard? Paul was her son too. Why didn't she take the whole knotted mess of spaghetti and throw it into the garbage? Paul still made no attempt to eat but sat hitting his shoe against the table leg.

"Paul," Richard said, "Mrs. McIntosh did not prepare this fine meal in order to have it thrown in the garbage. Not only is your refusal to eat a waste of good food, but it is bad manners." Richard looked at his watch. "I'll give you ten minutes. You either clean up your plate or I'll take you into the bathroom and give you a beating with my belt."

Now that he had played his hand, Richard stood up, picked up his coffee and started toward the living room sofa.

Tom was sitting in a basket chair. Leslie heard him say, "Not in my home you won't."

She was amazed that he would say anything so rash, to make a move before the winner was declared. There was still a chance, however slight, that Paul would finish his spaghetti. Tom wasn't waiting for that possibility; he'd been pushed too far. Leslie felt a peculiar thrill, strongly sexual, watching him. In their eight months of married life, she'd never seen him dig in this way.

Richard stopped in the middle of the sisal rug. He turned his head sideways. There was a half smile on his lips, a smile of incredulity. "What did you say?"

Tom got up out of the basket chair and faced Richard. "I said, not in my home you won't."

"Are you telling me how to bring up my own son?" He looked like he might hit Tom.

Tom folded his arms across his chest. "No, I'm not," he said quietly. "I'm merely telling you what I won't permit in my own home."

As the two men stood there staring at each other Leslie heard a tinny nasal voice — very faint — coming from downstairs.

Fish gotta swim, birds gotta fly,
I'm gonna love one man till I die.

And she started to laugh. She couldn't help it. Old Man Proctor's granddaughter was at it again. Leslie sat down in the basket chair. She was laughing so hard she had to hold onto her sides. Tears streamed down her cheeks. She didn't dare look at Tom.

Richard gave her an injured look. Very carefully, he set his coffee cup on the mantelpiece. "In that case, we'll go," he said. He motioned for Nancy and Charlotte to follow and jerked a thumb at Paul, who had his head down, a replica of his father's earlier smile on his face.

All three followed Richard into the hall and put on their coats.

Leslie pulled herself together and went into the bedroom for the library books, the colouring books and crayons. One of the new library books lay open on the bed. A thick black line had been crayoned across the shiny page.

After she had carried the books down the hall and given them to Nancy, Leslie got the candy centrepiece from the table and handed it to her as well. "Don't forget this," she said. "I'd like the kids to have it."

"No thanks," Nancy said stiffly. She turned and walked into the corridor.

Oh come *on*, Leslie felt like saying. Isn't that going too far? Instead she tried to apologize. "I'm sorry about the laughing. It was the girl downstairs." Leslie's voice faltered. "It's hard to explain."

Still Nancy said nothing but stood feet planted stolidly apart, eyes down, on her bulging belly.

As Leslie looked at her old friend, an incredible sadness swept over her, a heavy weight that came with wondering how much time this family, including the unborn child, would have to spend living down Richard's unhappy childhood.

"Good luck with the baby," Leslie said, "and everything."

"Thanks," Nancy finally said. And they were gone.

Leslie went into the living room. Through the heat register, she heard Fay's whiny voice reaching for the high notes.

When he goes awaaay, it's a rainy daaay,
But when he comes home again . . .

Tom was at the fireplace crumpling up newspaper, piling on wood scraps, relighting the fire. He looked awkward hunched over, his shirt-tail coming out of his trousers, his hair ruffled. Leslie watched him rummage in his pocket for a folder of matches, typically ignoring the box of elegantly long matches she had placed on the mantelpiece. She thought of going into the bedroom, taking the diaphragm out of her jewellery box, where she had hidden it from Old Man Proctor's prying eyes, putting on her sheer nightgown — but that was all she did, thought about it. She walked over to her husband and, unbuttoning his shirt and unzipping his trousers, she slowly undressed him. Then she made love to him in front of the fire, on the untidy heap of clothes she had dropped on the floor.

Salvation

Mary Anne stood at the kitchen sink holding the comb under the water so she could flatten her hair with it, feeling her mother's eyes on her the whole time. Lou sat bunched inside a terry-cloth bathrobe, tracing the flecks on the Arborite table and drinking tea. Mary Anne knew that the tea was to cure a hangover and to keep her mother awake. Her mother thought she didn't know about the hangover, or why she was so tired, but Mary Anne knew all right. She also knew why her mother kept getting up every Sunday to make breakfast when Mary Anne was quite capable of making it herself and did every other day of the week. Her mother was a fallen woman was why. She was having an affair with Corporal Simpson. It was true the Corporal's wife was in the insane asylum for the rest of her life, but he was still married to her, so being with her mother was wrong.

He was the third man her mother had taken up with since Mary Anne's father had died of a brain tumour ten years ago. Her mother had been brought up in the church; she knew she shouldn't be carrying on like this, but she wouldn't come to church and confess her sins. She figured that by getting Mary Anne's breakfast, it was enough.

"Why don't you come with me?" Mary Anne said.

"Now don't start that again," Lou said grumpily. "If you want to go, fine and dandy, but I have no intention of going to church. All they do is make you feel guilty about having fun. I work hard. I deserve what little fun I have." She stuck her worn mules out from beneath the table and rubbed her swollen ankles, a reminder that she'd been standing on them all day Saturday.

Mary Anne had heard all this before; how, after Rudy died, her mother had to go to work to support them. He had left the house, but that was all, so Lou had borrowed some money and went away to take a hairdressing course. While she was gone, Mary Anne's grandmother kept house and took Mary Anne to church — her grandmother never missed a Sunday. Her mother never went to church, not even after Mary Anne's grandmother had a stroke and couldn't take Mary Anne anymore.

After hairdressing school, Lou came back and opened up her own business — nothing fancy, but she had three operators working for her. It was true her mother worked hard, but that didn't excuse the other. Once Mary Anne overheard her grandmother and her mother having an argument. Lou was saying how worried she was about Mary Anne never going out with boys or being interested in clothes or movies. All she cared about was going to church and reading the Bible. It wasn't normal. At her age, Lou would have been crying her eyes out if she'd missed a dance. Mary Anne had been mad at her mother for saying that, but her grandmother had set her straight. She told Lou she'd be a lot better off if she mended her ways and took her daughter to church herself.

When Mary Anne's hair was wet enough to suit her, she pulled it back so tight it hurt her temples and secured it with an elastic.

"You keep watering it like that and it'll grow darker," Lou warned. Mary Anne ignored this remark.

"I can't figure it out," Lou went on. "Every week I've got customers coming into the shop asking me to dye their hair the same colour yours is, and what do you do? Darken it."

"I'm sure God doesn't care what colour my hair is," Mary Anne said primly.

"Did you ask Him?" Lou said. "Now there's an idea. I'm thinking of opening up a shop in Sheffield. Maybe I should ask God first."

Mary Anne glared at her mother. How dare she blaspheme the Lord? Her mother thought being blasphemous showed a sense of humour. She was always telling Mary Anne she should develop a sense of humour because it could get you through some rough times in your life. If having a sense of humour meant you mocked God, Mary Anne didn't want one.

"At least you get to wear that dress someplace," Lou was saying. "I had a lot of trouble with the pleats, you know. Are you wearing a bra?"

"I don't need a bra."

"True," Lou agreed. "You've got nothing to hold up. Still, a fourteen-year-old girl should wear one just to be feminine."

"Well, I'm not."

"When you get your periods," Lou said knowingly, "you'll develop breasts."

Really, her mother required so much patience. She was forever nagging her about menstruation. Did she have any questions? Did she want to talk about it? Mary Anne had known about menstruation since she was ten years old. She had read the booklet on it in the library from cover to cover. She didn't see what all the fuss was about. The subject was boring. All this stuff about developing breasts, having babies and bleeding, as if there was nothing else to think about.

Mary Anne took the two dollars she had earned babysitting at Foleys Friday night from the windowsill and put it in her purse, deliberately in front of her mother so it would be an example. "Do you want to give something?" she said. "There's a special collection today."

Lou took this in her stride. "Look. The wealthiest people in town go to church. They don't need my hard-earned money."

Mary Anne was tempted to remind her mother of the widow's mite, but what good would it do if her mother didn't care? Instead she said, "It would have been better spent in church than on liquor."

Every weekend, her mother bought a bottle of rum to drink when Corporal Simpson, Al, she called him, came over. Usually he came on Fridays, when Mary Anne babysat for the Foleys, but if he was on duty Friday, he came on Saturday night instead. They had a couple of drinks sitting in the front room with the TV turned up loud, trying to fool Mary Anne into thinking they were watching it. They weren't. What they were doing was gossiping. Bearing false witness, Reverend Notley called it. Being head of the RCMP detachment, Al knew all the dirty business in town, and her mother, being a hairdresser, was told all kinds of gossip. She once said that people must think she was a priest because they always treated an appointment like a confession. That was the way her mother talked about religion, always mocking it. That was why Mary Anne would never trust her with anything important. She knew her mother didn't know this was the reason she didn't confide in her; she thought it was because Mary Anne was quiet like her father had been.

Mary Anne didn't remember her father as being quiet. Maybe that was because what she mostly remembered was sitting on his knee and being bounced up and down until she laughed, and then he laughed too. His photograph on her bureau showed a young man, a boy almost, serious and sad. Mary Anne didn't know if he really had been serious and sad or whether it was because she wanted him to be. Once she'd asked Lou if he'd been a church-goer, wanting her to say yes, and Lou laughed unpleasantly and said, "Him? Only time he ever was in church was when were married."

After Lou and Al figured Mary Anne was asleep, they turned off the TV and went into Lou's bedroom. Mary Anne heard the door close and the bed thud against the wall. They thought that because she was upstairs and Lou downstairs, in what used to be the dining room, Mary Anne didn't know what was going on. She knew all right, and she couldn't get to sleep until she heard the toilet flush and the back door close, which was the signal that at last Corporal Simpson had gone home. Until he left, she had to lie there in her own bed and be punished for the sins being done on her mother's bed. It wasn't right, and if it made her mother mad to hear the truth, well, it was just too bad.

"Listen, Miss High-and-Mighty" — Lou had got up now and was balancing herself against the table with one hand and holding her bathrobe closed over her cleavage with the other, a pretty woman without softness — "don't you start telling me how to spend my money. I work hard to keep food in your mouth and decent clothes on your back. Do you have any idea why I'm staying in this dump? Do you think I want to slave away like this forever? I'm thirty-two years old, and if I don't want to spend Sundays on my knees, that's my business, not yours. Don't they teach you respect for your elders in that church?" She stumbled toward the door. "That's one of the Ten Commandments," she flung over her shoulder and went back to bed.

Mary Anne sat at the back of the church in the last pew, hard against the wood panelling. She always came to church half an hour early so she could look up the hymns ahead of time. It appealed to her sense of order and rightness, like making her bed as soon as she got out of it or returning a book to its shelf each night after she'd read it, even though it meant padding across the cold floor in her bare feet. She couldn't get to sleep if she left it on the night table.

After she had marked the hymns with Kleenex, she leaned back and looked around the church, composing herself, waiting, allowing the church's interior to seep into her own. The church was dimly lit, with dark hidden corners and tattered flags swaying over the heat register like ghost banners being marched into a battle by an army of Christian saints. Mary Anne liked the smell of the church, the little-changed air smelling mustily of all those who had breathed into it during years of Sunday services, Wednesday prayer meetings, weddings and funerals.

She sat alone. When her grandmother used to bring her, she marched Mary Anne right down to the front row, which embarrassed Mary Anne because everyone stared at them. That didn't bother her grandmother, who, before her stroke, had been as solid as a chunk of granite. When Mary Anne whispered, couldn't they sit at the back, her grandmother scoffed, "Nonsense, we've got nothing to hide. Good Christians must stand up and be counted."

People were moving erratically down the aisles now to the front pews. These were the born Baptists secure in their church-going, in what Reverend Notley called Christian fellowship. They smiled at one another, their broad smiles bolstered by gripping handshakes, and whispered sideways to one another, leaning their heads together. None of them acknowledged Mary Anne or even looked at her, and although she wanted to be alone, she didn't want to stand out in her aloneness as one scraggly tree on an island. To her relief, an old man she knew as Mr. Thomas came through the doorway and, with the intense concentration of the severely arthritic, lowered himself slowly onto the other end of the padded seat. He hooked his cane over the pew in front and groped in the rack for a hymnal; it fell to the floor. He left it there and picked up another. Mary Anne wondered if she should slide over and pick it up for him. If she did, he was sure to say something to her. She knew he was hard of hearing and spoke too loudly. Everyone would turn around and look at her. It occurred to her that God might be testing her, and she should pick it up. But she wasn't ready to risk the embarrassment and remained sitting where she was, her own hymnal in her lap.

The choir filed in, dressed in wine-coloured gowns that matched the pew cushions. When they were in place, Reverend Notley opened the door in the side wall of the choir loft, the door of the inner sanctum, a secret hollow near God's heart, and out stepped a second minister, one Mary Anne had never seen before. Reverend Notley looked stern and serious, very different from the way he looked outside the church. Whenever Mary Anne saw him downtown, he was smiling. He smiled at everyone whether or not they were Baptists. A short, wiry man, he had a tall, thin wife who had five daughters and another baby on the way. Mrs. Notley always looked ill, washed-out. Mary Anne had overheard a lady say after last Sunday's service that she was one of those poor souls who was sick every day of her pregnancy. Maybe that was God's way of punishing her for fornicating, which you had to do to have babies. Mary Anne had no intention of ever fornicating or having babies. She was going to be a missionary. Often she put herself to sleep at nights by imagining herself in white, ministering to the halt, the sick and the black, far-off from civilization.

Mary Anne could see Mrs. Notley in the front pew, but Reverend Notley didn't seem to notice her; he never looked at anyone in church. The minister with Reverend Notley was older, with grey hair and metal-rimmed glasses. He was beak-nosed and frightening. After the first hymn, Reverend Notley introduced the man as Dr. Richard Wallis from West End Baptist Church in Halifax. Soon after he was introduced, Dr. Wallis read the scripture: Luke 18, verses 18-30, which was the story of a certain ruler who asked Jesus what he must do to inherit eternal life. Jesus told him to sell everything he owned, for he was exceedingly rich, and give the money to the poor. The rich man could not do this and went away sad. The disciples asked Jesus, "Who then can be saved?" and Jesus said, "The things which are impossible with men are possible with God."

After the scripture, there were announcements, collection, another hymn and an anthem. Then Dr. Wallis stood up to give the sermon. He gripped the sides of the pulpit and leaned forward, staring at the congregation like a mighty eagle surveying the forest kingdom from his lofty nest.

"Today," he began, "I am going to bring you the message of joy, the joy of giving. The joy of giving oneself to God totally, completely, holding nothing back. Take the story of the rich man who came to Jesus. He wanted to be like Jesus. He wanted to lead a Christian life but he couldn't pay the price. It cost too much. The price," here Dr. Wallis paused emphatically, "the price, my friends, was *too high*! But it isn't money we use to become good Christians. That is why Jesus told the rich man to get rid of his money. The currency we use is ourselves. Our souls, my friends, these are what Jesus wants." Dr. Wallis's voice was strong and resonant, and Mary Anne felt it echoing inside her head.

"To give ourselves to Jesus, we must first be cleansed by acknowledging our sin, our own personal sin, for we are *all* born in sin and, without Jesus' help, we die in sin. But" — Dr. Wallis paused again and pointed one finger in the air, slightly backwards and to one side, like a teacher chalking GOD on the blackboard for his pupils to see — "God knows this. He understands. He loves us. Loves *us*. Isn't that wonderful? So He sent His only begotten Son into the world to *save* us. Save each and every one of us. That is the miracle of Jesus. To save sinners like ourselves from ourselves!"

Mary Anne heard someone up front say, "Yes. Yes." No one in Reverend Notley's sermons had ever done that. His sermons were quiet and sometimes hard to understand. They were never as strong and clear as this. Mr. Thomas was moving around at the end of the pew. He was nodding his head up and down, agreeing with the minister.

Dr. Wallis's voice rose, and raising himself onto the balls of his feet, he spoke as if he were angry at everyone and at Mary Anne personally. Was he angry because he knew she hadn't been saved?

"God is not asking us to take on the guilt of mankind. We cannot take on the sins of others. All He is asking is for each one of us to confess his own sins. Here. Today. The miracle is that each of us is a gift, a unique gift, a gift no one else can duplicate. Now we don't give each other gifts wrapped in soiled paper, do we? We use new paper. It's the same thing when we give ourselves to God. Before we make our gift, we must confess our sins, purify ourselves, make ourselves new. Then we are ready to be saved!"

Dr. Wallis pounded the pulpit with his fist. "What we are going to do right now is to bow our heads and pray to God for our forgiveness. After we pray, we will wait in silence for the healing power of His love to flow through us. Those who want to throw off their yokes of sin, those who want to give themselves to Jesus can step forward. Then we can rejoice in their salvation. Let us pray."

Mary Anne bowed her head, released from Dr. Wallis's fierce stare; his eagle eyes pierced through her, seeing what she hadn't been able to see herself. She knew her mother's sins had made her feel unworthy. But hadn't Dr. Wallis plainly said you couldn't take on the sins of others? All this time she had been weighed down by her mother's sins. She felt guilty for the two of them. That was why she hadn't been saved. And she couldn't be baptized until she'd been saved. Sometimes during services, Reverend Notley asked those people who'd been saved to get up in front of the congregation and talk about it. Witnessing, he called it. Mary Anne envied these people for the way they sang and shouted, praising the Lord in their joyousness. She wanted to experience that joy and, until now, had never understood that it had been denied her because she had never thought of herself as a gift before. All she had to do now was to confess her own sins and give herself to Jesus. Once she was purified, He would take her. What had once been beyond her understanding was now so simple and clear. As Dr. Wallis said, the things that are impossible with men are possible with God.

She closed her eyes and concentrated on her own sins. She was in the habit of stealing Mrs. Foley's baking goods when she was babysitting. She didn't know why she did this. Her mother kept the same supplies at home, but she never touched them. But always on Friday nights, after the Foleys had gone out and she had read the twins a story, she'd sneak into the kitchen, going directly to the cupboard over the stove where the baking supplies were. One by one, she opened up the bags of walnuts, raisins, currants and chocolate chips. She never took many, only a few from each bag, putting them back exactly where they had been so that Mrs. Foley wouldn't be able to tell. She never drank the bottle of Coke Mrs. Foley left for her as if, by not taking it, it was all right to take the baking goods. But it wasn't right. It was stealing. She pressed her hands together tightly and asked God for His forgiveness. And for the time she'd taken the book on Albert Schweitzer from the school library, deliberately taken it and not signed it out. Monica wanted it for a report she was writing. Had to have it, she said, and nearly cried when she couldn't find it. Mary Anne had slipped it inside her binder. She returned it the next week after she'd read it and the reports had been passed in. Mary Anne wasn't assigned a report, but why shouldn't she have the book? After all, she was the one planning to become a missionary, not Monica. Monica was one of those who smoked in the washroom, swore and went out with boys. Now Mary Anne understood that by keeping the book, she had been guilty of selfishness. Fidgeting blindly with her Kleenex, she prayed she'd be forgiven so she could be saved. She remembered Mr. Thomas's hymnal. Opening her eyes, she quickly slid across the pew, picked up the hymnal from the floor and returned it to the rack. As she eased back to her place, she felt a stab of pain in her stomach, then a slight wetness between her legs. She felt strangely heavy, almost too tired to sit up. She closed her eyes, swaying in an effort to stay upright. She couldn't hear Dr. Wallis's voice anymore which meant the prayer had stopped. The moment of silence had begun, the time for being forgiven.

There was a clumsy shuffling at the end of the pew. Mr. Thomas was moving around. His cane clattered to the floor. She thought she could hear him going down the aisle. Still she dared not open her eyes, afraid that if she did too soon, before she was ready, she might be denied her salvation. There was one more sin to confess, and that was the picture of her mother and Al lying naked in bed, fornicating. When they were doing it, the picture of them was so real that she had to pull the sheets up over her head, and still she couldn't blot it out. Reverend Notley had once said that people can commit adultery in their minds, which was as bad as doing it. She prayed to God to forgive her for imagining it. With God's help, she would push that picture out of her mind. Her mother's sins had nothing to do with her, even if she got a baby out of it. Her mother would have to look after her own salvation.

There was a shout from the front of the church, then another. Mary Anne recognized Dr. Wallis's voice. "God be praised!" he was saying.

Mary Anne opened her eyes and looked to the front. Mr. Thomas was walking back and forth in front of the pulpit without his cane. He was smiling at the congregation, lifting his legs high like a soldier proud of his new uniform. "I'm saved! I'm saved!" he shouted over and over, and some of the people replied, "God be praised!"

Dr. Wallis was smiling now and shouting above the din. "Is there anyone else who wants to feel God's power by giving herself to Jesus?"

He scanned the congregation and his eyes fell on Mary Anne. As she sat under his brutal stare, two bright spots appeared on her cheeks. Her eyes were riveted to his and she knew that her time had come. She had confessed her sins; she was ready. She forgot the pain, the wetness, the heaviness; she forgot her shyness, she forgot her guilt. All of it came up out of her, thrusting upward, lifting her heart up until she found herself on her feet with her arms over her head.

"I want to give myself to Jesus!" she shouted. "I want to give myself to Jesus!"

"God be praised!" Dr. Wallis shouted back. He held out his arms. "Come forward, my child. Come forward. God's arms will protect you."

Mary Anne stumbled out of the pew and down the aisle to the front. Dr. Wallis came down from the platform and caught her as she reached the pulpit. Her chest was tight with the pressure of joy inside it. Now she really belonged to Jesus. She began to cry for the freedom she felt and for the joyousness flowing through her, knowing at last that Jesus loved her, that His gentle eyes were on her soul, which was as clean and unblemished as a newborn's. Now she was ready to be baptized.

Dr. Wallis put the hymnal in her hand, open at the right page, but she could scarcely see the words through the happy tears. She heard Dr. Wallis's strong voice beside her and the congregation singing full out, racing ahead of the organ's slow thundering. As the people sang, she felt as if her heart would burst with gladness, and she soared up to the heights of glory where saints and angels sang.

When the benediction had been given, Dr. Wallis embraced her, and Reverend Notley came down to shake her hand. Old folks from the front pew came forward to pat her on the back. Mary Anne wiped her eyes and blew her nose. She felt drained, weak, now that it was all over, and full of what she took to be God's peace. There was nothing more to do, so she drifted up the aisle, allowing the congregation to move her along like the Virgin being borne on the shoulders of pilgrims.

Outside, people stood in knots of conversation on the pavement. As always, they ignored Mary Anne. She drifted past them to the sidewalk and started in the direction of home. It wasn't until she was within a block of the house that she became completely aware of the dampness between her legs; still she didn't quicken her pace.

Once she was inside the house, she went straight to the bathroom. With the same disinterest she had once given to undressing her doll, she took off her pants and saw a red stain in the crotch. She twisted around and saw two pleats of her white dress were red.

She opened Lou's bedroom door; as expected, her mother was still in bed.

"There's blood in my pants," Mary Anne announced.

Lou sat upright. "Well, well," she grinned and swung her legs over the side of the bed. "Your period at last. It's about time. Go to the bathroom and wait for me."

Obediently, Mary Anne went into the bathroom. While Lou rummaged in her lingerie drawer for a belt and pads, she saw the book and placed it on the bed. It was now or never. You couldn't have your daughter menstruating and not knowing what was what.

After Mary Anne was fixed up and the white dress put to soak in the bathtub, her mother sat her down on the bed and went over the book with her. She even got a piece of paper and a pencil and drew pictures to make it clearer. Throughout all this, Mary Anne sat quietly on the edge of the bed. She didn't ask questions; she didn't say she already knew about menstruation but let her mother explain it. It didn't occur to Mary Anne that her mother might interpret this acquiescence as a need for motherly support.

"Some girls are frightened at first by the idea of blood coming out of them." Lou said warmly. "But it's perfectly normal. You mustn't be frightened." She reached over and pulled Mary Anne closer.

Mary Anne allowed this embrace, but she didn't tell her mother that she wasn't frightened. Nor did she tell her the real reason for beginning to menstruate on this special day, the day she had given herself to Jesus. Her mother would never know that the blood was a sign from God, a symbol of her salvation.

Territory

Florence McDermott was in the back lane, a narrow strip of road and grass at the rear of her lot, one of thousands of squares in Calgary's geometric grid. Florence disliked living on a grid. She felt surrounded, suffocated and, at times, under siege. To protect herself and her family, she put up high walls; a vertical-slatted fence she painted white every third summer. Within this fence was her house, a neat white box with white trim that was nine years short of being paid for. Florence picked up a disposable diaper from the lane, carried it to the trash can, lifted the lid and dropped it inside. The diaper wasn't from her garbage; her children were well past that stage. Dogs had dragged it here. She picked up a bloodied Kotex pad, also someone else's. Fortunately, she was wearing rubber gloves.

An old lady whom Florence didn't know — she wasn't from this neighbourhood but several streets over on the grid — went past, walking her poodle on the sidewalk. The poodle was blind and led with his nose, pulling the old woman behind on the leash.

The old woman carried a paper bag and a child's plastic spade to clean up his droppings.

"Terrible thing the way people leave their messes around these days," she remarked.

"It certainly is," Florence agreed.

"If everyone would do his job, this world would be a lot better place to live in," the old woman said. She stopped while the dog lifted his leg against Florence's fence post.

This was exactly what Florence was trying to teach her children. And it was what her father, a small-town minister who was now dead, had taught her. Accountability had been the mainstay of numerous sermons. But Florence didn't invite the old woman to say more, nor did she look closely at the old woman beyond noticing that she was wearing a black coat. Florence didn't have time for idle chit-chat.

"Should get your kids to do that," the old woman advised. "Kids don't have enough work to do as it is. Not like the old days, when everyone had chores."

Florence didn't want to hear about the old days. Normally her son Bruce looked after the garbage, and Florence was only doing it today because there were some things she didn't want his child's eyes to see. The Kotex pad, for instance.

"Or your husband," the old woman said.

Florence knew she was fishing, but she said, to let it be known that there was a husband, "He's up north working on an oil rig."

"Must be hard for you," the old woman said; then, when Florence didn't reply, she muttered, "Riff-raff, that's what I call people who let their dogs run loose, getting into other people's garbage."

Florence didn't take her up on this either. She bent over and picked up a torn plastic bag and put it in the trash can. The poodle strained on the leash, and the old woman allowed herself to be led away.

Though Florence avoided words like *riff-raff* and *trash* that betrayed snobbishness, she had to agree, the old woman was on the right track.

The dogs who had dragged the garbage here came from a house four squares up the grid, on the other side of the lane. It was a house that had been rented to a succession of transients including, as of a month ago, a woman with two mongrel dogs and a little girl named Marcy. Marcy had materialized on Florence's doorstep one day calling for her daughter Amanda. Flimsily dressed against the winter cold, Marcy had a milk-pale face, nested hair and eyes as sad as a painted Jesus. Since then, the child had come to their house nearly every day to play with Amanda's dolls, watch TV, cuddle Bruce's rabbits. She was an unobtrusive little girl who worked hard at staying out of Florence's way.

Florence hadn't met Marcy's mother, though she had been intending to. As one of a diminishing population of women who were staying home to look after children, she made it a point of visiting newcomers who moved into the immediate neighbourhood, though recently, with FOR SALE signs springing up overnight like winter mushrooms, she wondered if this wasn't a lost cause. There was nothing frivolous about these visits; she felt it her responsibility to know the parents of her children's friends. Now she had another reason for meeting Marcy's mother, who should be told about her dogs getting into the garbage.

Before going into the house, Florence went into the yard and checked the rabbit cage for droppings. The cage was dirty, and she would have to remind Bruce to clean it out after school. When she returned to the kitchen, she rinsed the gloves under the hot water tap and hung them under the sink on a clothespin she kept there especially for that purpose. Then she washed her hands and, drying them on a paper towel, looked around her immaculate kitchen. Noticing Bruce's fingerprints on the white wall behind the table, she wet a paper towel, wiped off the marks and put the towel in the garbage bag. Florence liked to keep up with small jobs, she didn't like housework to pile up. She checked her watch: eleven o'clock. If she visited Marcy's mother now, she'd be back in time to make her children their lunch. She went into the bathroom, looked into the mirror and combed her hair. Then she put on her Hudson's

Bay coat, buttoned it up and went out the back door; she seldom used the front door in order not to soil the beige broadloom.

The house Marcy lived in was a brown bungalow with a broken picture window at the front. There was a USE THE BACK DOOR sign on the door. Obediently, Florence went around the back, avoiding the two mongrels snapping and growling at each other on the feces-stained snow. She pushed open the broken gate, went past the overturned pails, the rusted car, hood up, parked on what in summer would have been lawn. The back door was ajar so Florence stepped tentatively inside and yoo-hooed. There was no answer. She heard a muffled laugh from somewhere deep inside the house. That must be Marcy's mother. She took three steps up and yoo-hooed again. While she waited, she looked around.

In front of her, half a dozen paper bags darkened with circles of grease and bulging with saw-toothed cans, leaned into each other. The table and countertop were littered with unwashed dishes, beer bottles and overturned milk cartons. Although Florence was so tidy she sometimes put out a hand to remove Derrick's plate before he finished eating from it — her husband was a slow eater — she wasn't offended by the mess because it didn't belong to her. In fact, she almost enjoyed looking at a mess she wasn't accountable for. It occurred to her that this freedom to stare un-observed at someone else's mess was an invasion of privacy, and she yoo-hooed again, louder this time. The loudness of her voice jolted her into the guilty realization that perhaps she had deliber-ately kept her voice too soft when she had called before in order to gain more time to look around.

"Coming!" a voice sang out and a woman burst into the kitch-en in a kimono. She was pursued by a naked, hairy man with a green towel fig-leafed over his genitals and a face cloth on his head. He pranced around in a circle wiggling his buttocks, hands flapping in mid-air.

"Cut it out, Arnie!" The woman was bent double, laughing. "Quit putting on the dog. We've got company."

"Maybe I'd better come back some other time," Florence said. She felt an obscure anger that came not from censure but from envy. It reminded her how often she had longed to be free-wheeling like this and never could be.

"No, you stay. Arnie and me were just foolin' around. We'll quit." The woman gave his buttocks a swat. "Shoo," she said.

Arnie pranced toward Florence, gave the green towel a flick, then ran in mock horror out of the kitchen and down the hall.

Florence was irritated by his impudence, but this had not prevented her from staring at the dark, bushy V between his legs.

The woman straightened her kimono and faced Florence.

"Who are you?" she said.

"I'm Florence McDermott, Amanda's mother."

The woman frowned. "Who?"

"Amanda's mother. Your little girl, Marcy, plays at my house."

"Oh yeah," the woman said. "Sure. Come on in."

Florence advanced a step.

"My name's Vi. Here," the woman shoved a chair toward Florence, "take the load off your feet."

Florence sat on the edge of the chair, carefully, so her back wouldn't touch.

"Just a sec," Vi said.

She padded barefoot across the room, reached under a Corn Flakes box and retrieved her cigarettes. She pulled one out, went over to the stove, turned on the front burner and bent over the blue flame to light her cigarette. She did this slowly, as if she was enjoying the ritual, knowing she was being watched.

Vi had dirty toenails, lank brown hair pushed behind her ears and eyebrows plucked thin too soon. She looked older than Florence, who was thirty-five, but Florence was sure she was much younger. She didn't know why she thought this. It had to do with the quick way Vi jerked back from the flame, the starving animal cunningly avoiding a steel trap, the hard, tight lines creasing the corners of her mouth when she took the first puff; the skill with which she inhaled suggested other worldly accomplishments mastered early. Vi didn't offer a cigarette, not that Florence smoked, but sometimes she accepted one just to be sociable.

Vi leaned against the counter. "So what can I do for you?"

Florence was acutely aware of her dry-cleaned slacks and washed hair. "I just came over to say hi. You know, welcome you to the neighbourhood."

"Oh yeah. You live around the corner somewhere." Vi took a drag, keeping her eyes on the jet trails she was expertly exhaling. "You're the one with the rabbits, aren't you?"

"They're my son's."

"Marce goes on and on about them rabbits. Wants one, I guess."

Although this was said in a resigned way as if it was just one of a long list of unreasonable requests, Florence accepted it as a hint. "Well, if they have a litter, I'll let you know."

"Sure," Vi took one final drag, exhaled, then dropped her cigarette into a beer bottle.

"While I'm here I'd like to get your phone number," Florence said. "Just in case. You never know."

Vi wandered into the front hall and came back with a used envelope and a pencil stub. When she leaned over the table to write down the number, Florence saw her breasts hang forward, twinned together like matching udders. Vi looked up speculatively, caught Florence's eyes before they could shift but made no effort to cover herself up.

"What's yours?"

Florence gave her the number; they exchanged paper scraps.

"It was real friendly of you to come over. I been in Vegas so long I forgot people did this," Vi said.

Florence seized this opening. She was unabashedly curious. Staying at home as she did, she had to pick up tidbits wherever they'd been tossed, like a gull in a parking lot. "You're from Las Vegas, are you?"

"Yeah. Came up here to get away from my ex. Wouldn't stop pesterin' me. First he deserts, then he pesters. Had to leave a good job at Caesar's to get away from him. You been there?"

"No, but I'd like to." Florence's mental picture of Vegas was slot machines, busty cocktail waitresses, spotlit stars, people on the make between marriages. It was a den of iniquity she was curious to see from a safe distance, with her husband. The reason she didn't think she could trust herself to visit Sodom and Gomorrah alone was that when she thought of such places, she sometimes caught glimpses of herself flinging her clothes onto casino tables, dancing in drunken splendour, sprawling naked on velvet cushions in smoke-filled rooms, challenging all comers. These glimpses were as far as she got before she turned herself into a pillar of salt with a bolt of guilt.

"You'll probably find this city tame by comparison," Florence said.

"Oh no. My job at Blackbeard's keeps me hopping. Pay's not as good. But" — she grinned at Florence — "men are the same everywhere, if you get what I mean."

Florence, whose experience could neither confirm nor deny this statement, nevertheless tried. "I guess that's right," she said. Then, with the same awkwardness, added, "By the way, your dogs are getting into our garbage. I wonder if you'd keep them in your yard or tie them up."

Vi gave her a shrewd look that said *so that's why you came.* But she was agreeable enough. "They're not my dogs. They're my boyfriend's," she said. "I'll tell him."

"Thanks," Florence said, then, relieved to have gotten than over with, she stood up and said, "I must get home and make lunch." She went to the door. "Now if there's anything I can do for you, let me know."

"I will," Vi promised.

After Florence had closed the door behind her and stepped onto the snow, a red-haired, bearded man she hadn't noticed before stuck his head out from under the car hood and waved at her. A second man. Apparently Vi lived not with one man but two. Though this thought gave her a certain vicarious pleasure, Florence made a mental note not to let Amanda play here. Not because of the mess and the filth but the men. And Vi's freewheeling casualness. In a small town, Little Red Riding Hood knew which road not to take to Grandma's, but in a city like Calgary, the Big Bad Wolf drove around in cars, stalked parks and shopping malls, moved in and out of neighbourhoods.

The dogs were waiting for her on the sidewalk. One of the mongrels, a dirty white brute with shag fur and small pig eyes, jumped up on her. The other one, a smaller black dog with patches of tea-brown spilt all over it and a narrow, wolfish face, came up from behind, sniffing her legs. Never having had a dog, even as a child, Florence was timid with them, but today she pushed the dogs roughly aside. Neither dog was discouraged, and they followed unnervingly close to her heels, so close that, when she reached her house and was unlatching the gate, the white dog streaked past her into the backyard before she could close the gate. The dog went straight to the rabbit cage. It made a wild, excited leap for the hutch, snapping its jaws against the chicken wire. The three rabbits bolted into the hutch, and the dog changed its strategy, tearing at the wooden door. Florence yelled at the dog but it did no good. She ran to the back steps, grabbed the broom she used for sweeping snow off the deck and hit the dog hard on its hindquarters. It snarled, yelped, retreated toward the gate. Florence unlatched the gate and shoved the dog out of the yard.

"Miserable beast," she muttered. She felt like going back to Vi's, finding whichever boyfriend owned the animals and telling him to tie up his wretched dogs *right now*, but of course she didn't. It amounted to nagging, which she tried to avoid, knowing her own impatience sometimes made her unreasonable. Give them a day or two, she told herself, and, in the meantime, warn the children to secure the gate latch.

Two days later, the dogs were still around, and Florence felt justified in phoning back. Vi answered the phone.

"I told my boyfriend about the dogs," Vi said. "He's going to fix the fence as soon as he's done the car."

"And when will that be?" Florence was careful to keep the sarcasm out of her voice, to maintain a safe, non-interfering neutral.

"Oh, one of these days," Vi said.

Florence could almost hear the shrug over the phone.

Then Vi asked if Marce could eat over at lunchtime for the next week. Because of her being new on the job, the manager had put her on the noon shift, the bastard, after she'd especially asked for nights, when tips were better and Marce was in bed. She'd make Marce a sandwich and send her over with it, if that was okay with Florence. Florence couldn't very well say no. After all, Vi was merely taking her at her word.

That same week, Florence came home from school, where she did occasional volunteer work, and found Bruce in the backyard cradling his favourite rabbit. He didn't respond when she called out, so she went over to him. Then she saw. The bloodied nose, the swollen upper lip, the cheek already puffed out and turning blue, the report card crumpled up in the snow. He wouldn't look, wouldn't answer questions but hid his face in the white fur.

She knew anyway. Celina Ratchford's brothers had caught her the same way. They grabbed her report card as she was walking home through the vacant lot behind the manse. There were three of them, Royce leading. They dragged her to a big elm tree and tied her. Masters of torture, they took their time peeling willow switches. For every A she got three whips across the legs, for every B two. It didn't matter how much she begged, how hard she cried. They urinated on her skirt. By the time they'd untied her, she'd wet herself. There are some people, her father had told her afterwards, who can't stand to see someone make something of herself, but this wasn't much help. Since then, Florence had come to understand this attack in terms of territory: the Notleys were Baptist, the Ratchfords were Catholic.

But it was her father's comfort she now offered Bruce, not because she believed it but because those were the only words that came to mind. Bruce kept his face hidden, refusing consolation. Florence went inside and eventually Bruce followed, driven by the arrival of his sister, who bounced home as springy as a new rubber ball with Marcy and two other friends. Amanda collected playmates the way Bruce collected stamps and coins. He was so studious, so comfortable with books instead of friends that Florence was relieved by the devotion he showed his rabbits.

He was sitting on his bed fiddling with the tiny drawers of his coin collection when she came into his bedroom. "Who were they?" she wanted to know.

He wouldn't answer. His cheek was swollen to the size of a golf ball.

Florence went into the kitchen, made up an ice pack and, when she came back with it, tried again. "Look, if I knew who they were I could phone the school and report them."

"It didn't happen at school."

"When then?"

"Behind the drugstore."

"Well then, I'll phone their parents."

"No."

"Why not? They shouldn't be allowed to get away with this."

"They told me" — he stopped, the words came out thickly — "they told me if I didn't tell they'd leave me alone."

"But that's not fair," Florence said. "Don't you see?"

He looked up then. "Please Mum," he said, "leave me alone."

On Saturday, after breakfast on one of Derrick's weekends home, Marcy turned up at the door, hatless, in a sweater, shivering in the March wind. Amanda asked her inside to play.

At noontime, Florence told Marcy she'd have to go home now; they were going out this afternoon.

"I can't," Marcy piped in her Little Match Girl voice. "My mother said not to come home before five."

"And why not?"

"She's sleeping."

So Marcy came with them to the museum. Derrick was annoyed. He wasn't home that many weekends. Was it too much to expect to have his own family to himself?

When they got back from their outing, Derrick was further irritated to find their previous night's chicken bones spread over the driveway with most of the week's garbage. Florence told him the dogs were owned by one of Vi's boyfriends. Derrick went up the back lane and spoke to the red-haired man, whom he found where Florence had seen him, beneath the hood of his car.

"I told him to tie up his dogs or I'd report them," he told Florence afterwards.

"And?"

"He said he'd tie them until he gets his fence fixed."

"Why didn't he tie them when I complained to Vi?" She still had the idea, left over from her librarian days, that men got quicker results from their complaints than women did.

"You're not forceful enough, that's your problem," Derrick said. "Take that woman, for instance, she should be reported to the authorities for dumping her kid on you like this. You're not doing the kid a favour, you know, covering for her mother all the time."

"Somebody has to."

"Do-gooder."

Though she knew Derrick was teasing her about being a minister's daughter, it rankled. Florence had seen enough inept do-gooders to know why they had such a bad reputation. It was all very well for Derrick to advise, but he was away most of the time. He wasn't here at lunch to see Marcy's expectant face when she turned up with Amanda, or how grateful she was for the slightest favour. It wasn't any trouble giving her a glass of milk and an apple. And the situation wasn't that cut and dried. For one thing, Vi had to work and probably couldn't afford a babysitter, and for another, Marcy was fond of Vi. She talked about her a lot, bragging about Vi's new backless dress, how many boyfriends she had, how sometimes they took her to a drive-in movie with them. No matter how freewheeling Vi was, maybe the mother Marcy loved was better than some strange, though responsible, foster parent, which is probably what Marcy would get if the authorities were called. Besides, who was she to judge Vi? Florence knew she was being wishy-washy; she suspected herself of cowardice. She put the situation down to one of the occupational hazards of staying at home. And the situation wouldn't last forever. It was bound to change. In the meantime, she continued to feed Marcy lunches, gave her clothes Amanda had outgrown and took her in when she was locked out.

The dogs struck when Derrick was away. It was during the night, which explained why the sound of squealing rabbits went unheard. Bruce, on his way out the door with his school books, discovered the carnage. A magpie was already pecking at the rabbit's half-eaten body lying in the bloodied snow. Florence heard the cry, the books thud against the step, the magpie flapping away, squawking and indignant. Outside in her slippers, she saw the other two rabbits stretched out limp, necks broken. Bruce hadn't touched them. Hadn't moved from the foot of the steps. Simply stood there blinking, unable to believe what he was seeing. Florence went over to him and tried to put an arm around him, but he pushed her away. She walked around the yard trying to figure out how the dogs had managed to get at the rabbits. Judging from the deep tooth marks in the wood and the boards pried free of their nails, she surmised the dogs had chewed the boards loose enough to rip them off and get at the rabbits inside. At the last minute, the rabbits must have leaped through the opening because the snow was criss-crossed with their tracks and those of the dogs pursuing them around the yard. Florence followed the dog tracks across the yard to the fence. The dogs had loosened two fence slats to get into the yard. Florence hitched up her housecoat and nightgown, climbed over the fence and followed the dog tracks up the rectangular strip of lane. The tracks led straight to Vi's house. Florence banged loudly on the door, resisting the urge to kick it in. She would get them out of bed if it was the last thing she did.

But Vi was up. She opened the door almost at once and stood there in a short skirt and tight sweater, her face immobilized beneath old makeup.

"Your dogs," Florence bit off the words. "They've killed my son's rabbits."

"I told you," Vi's voice came out flat and stale. "They're not my dogs. They're my boyfriend's."

"I don't care whose they are. They belong to someone who lives in this house. And they killed my son's rabbits. They broke through our fence last night and ripped apart the hutch."

"Why didn't you build a stronger fence?" Vi challenged her. "Why didn't you make a better hutch? Even my old man could build a hutch. Everyone knows dogs go after rabbits." Having found an opening, Vi ducked through. "On the farm, my kid brother kept rabbits. Dogs never got 'em because me old man . . ."

"Don't you try to get out of it!" Florence snapped back. "*Those* dogs had no business being in *my* yard. I'm calling the dog pound and having them picked up immediately."

"You do that," Vi said and shut the door in her face.

Anger burned in Florence like acid in the womb. Rude, ignorant, she paused in the snow, then spat out the word, *slut*. The shock of using this word made her look up at the grey sky as if her father was up there watching behind a one-way window of smoked glass. Why didn't you tell me this? she railed at him. Why didn't you preach about people like this, people who will take everything you're willing to give, suck you dry and give back nothing in return? "It isn't fair," she said aloud, "it isn't fair." She wondered why it was that people are born expecting life to be fair and go right on expecting it. But then she thought: I brought this on myself. I left myself open for being used. And she resumed walking.

By the time Florence got home, Bruce had locked himself in his room. She got Amanda off to school and went outside, shovelled the rabbits into a Glad Bag and phoned the dog pound.

An hour later, when the dog catcher came around, Florence gave him the Glad Bag and Vi's house number. She had little confidence that he would catch the dogs, but she thought it was worth a try. Like rogue highwaymen, the worst dogs were wise to the ways of the law enforcers; they knew when it was prudent to loll about in their own backyards and when they could get away with plundering garbage. She saw the two mongrels up the lane later that afternoon; the white one's fur was streaked with dried rabbit blood. This time when she phoned the dog catcher, she was low-keyed but forceful so she couldn't possibly be dismissed as a hysterical housewife. The dog catcher told her the woman denied the dogs were hers. Not true, Florence informed him, or at least beside the point. The dogs belonged to the people living in that house. She made it clear she expected the dogs to be picked up that day or else. She didn't say what the "or else" was.

Had Derrick been home the problem might have been solved differently. He might have insisted on taking Vi's boyfriend to court. But he was away for three weeks this stretch, and she wasn't going to wait that long. And anyway, this was her territory. Derrick had his, up north where she couldn't go. And she didn't want to run to Derrick every time she had a problem. The problem was that she had promised Bruce a trip to the Pet Farm this weekend after Sunday school to buy baby rabbits, and the dogs had to be out of the way by then. She wanted the dog catcher to get the mongrels because that was his job. She thought of him as an institution she should be able to depend on so she could go inside her house, mind her own business and do her job.

Of course, if the dog catcher didn't do his job — here Florence hesitated — she was on shaky ground, ground that she knew her father, for all his sermonizing, would never sanctify. She pushed past this thought. If the dog catcher didn't come and get the mongrels by Thursday morning, if he didn't do his job, then she would be forced to take the matter into her own hands.

On Thursday morning, after sighting the dogs across the street, she drove to the hardware store, where she spent a long time in the pesticide section, finally choosing a weed poison, an especially potent dandelion killer a neighbour with a perfect lawn had recommended. Florence had never been able to use the poison herself; somehow she saw it as a violation of her past, those carefree girlhood hours she had spent with five sisters weaving milky dandelion stems into bracelets, blowing wishes on their puffballs. Here, within the city's geometric grid, dandelions weren't permitted this season of grace. Homeowners were expected to vaccinate their lawns against this plague of yellow-spotted fever or risk a fifty-dollar fine.

Florence took the dandelion killer and a pair of rubber gloves to the checkout and paid for them. Then she went to the supermarket and bought two pounds of chuck steak. She took the steak home, cut it into large chunks, dissolved the dandelion killer in a bucket of hot water and added the meat. Then she put a board over the bucket and hid it in the tool shed behind the lawn mower. As she walked into her house, Florence saw the old woman in the black coat come by with her poodle, but she ignored her.

That night, after her children were asleep, Florence went outside. She found the dogs in the back lane, for once in their own garbage. She acted swiftly, clearly, getting the bucket out of the tool shed, carrying it up the back lane, throwing the chunks of meat onto the snow. She didn't wait for the dogs to pounce on it before going home. She had the sense to take the bucket with her. Because, by this time, it had occurred to her that if Vi and her boyfriend found out it was she who had poisoned the dogs, they might try suing her; people sued on the slightest pretext these days. She certainly couldn't leave the bucket in the trash can; trash cans were always open to the explorations of children. She took the bucket home to her kitchen and washed it out. She used new rubber gloves, detergent, paper towels. She burned the paper towels in the fireplace and threw the rubber gloves into the garbage. Afterwards, she cleaned the sink with Ajax and put the bucket away. She went into the bathroom, washed her hands and patted her hair. She didn't look in the mirror.

Then she went downstairs to the family room, a square room with a low ceiling and no windows, and turned on the TV. She watched the flickering square of light announce a Julie Andrews special. Florence saw the singer's face, the clear eyes, the flawless skin, the red mouth opening and closing, but she didn't hear the music. She made no attempt to turn up the volume but sat there in Derrick's La-Z-Boy chair, rocking herself in the darkened womb of the basement.

The Holy Roller
Empire

Once it occurred to Alice that maybe she had stayed home and looked after her children longer than was necessary, she went out and joined the Holy Rollers. This wasn't a religious group but an artist's co-operative that was renting what had once been a laundry in order to obtain cheap studio space. The arrangement suited both the artists and the city, who planned on eventually tearing down the old laundry to make way for a road interchange.

Because she was a potter, Alice's space was a basement corner near the communal kiln. Outside her window was a shrub rooted between slabs of cement and suffocated with litter. Alice went outside and picked a cigarette package and a paper cup out of its branches. The shrub grew on one side of the driveway; on the other side was a brick building identical to the laundry; beyond that the concrete and glass skyscrapers of Calgary. The shrub reminded Alice of a tree outside the big old Maritime house where she had first learned to shape clay. She had worked in front of a bay window against a sky so white and flat it seemed a sheet of paper had been suspended over the diked marshlands.

After she had paid the Holy Rollers a month's rent, Alice went home, got into her blue jeans, hiking boots, sweater, put the roof rack on her bashed-in Volkswagen and drove to the lumberyard. With the baby bonus cheque — which she considered housewife's pay — she was going to buy two-by-fours and plywood for partitions. A metal sculptor, Lorne Harlan, had the open space in the basement corner opposite her. Alice wanted a closed-in space. She wanted a room with a door on which she could slap a KEEP OUT sign, something she couldn't do at home. As long as the sign came down at night, her husband Gib wouldn't mind. But Alice thought her children would take the sign as a rejection. She knew she had overindulged them, but she wasn't used to putting her interests first and felt she had to go away to do it, like a bitten animal licking its sores. Besides, there wasn't a place left in their bungalow for a studio, the cement walls in the basement having been wood panelled and the floor shagged over to make a re-creation room.

Gib offered her the station wagon to transport the lumber. Alice declined; the station wagon was for outings to the A&W, McDonald's. Now that she was dividing herself in two, there must be no overlapping of parts. Gib offered to help build her studio; again she declined. Though she had never pounded anything but picture nails into walls, she got the partitions up and the door in. It took her two weeks.

Masked in goggles, Lorne Harlan spent those weeks in the opposite corner welding together what appeared to be the remains of a car wreck with a blow torch. From time to time, Alice would glance over and see coils, wheels, pieces of scrap metal merge into a landscape of jagged cliffs and cratered canyons.

After she had moved in her tools, tables, slabs of clay, Alice went out and hiked along alleyways, past garbage pails, over vacant lots, picking up rusty nails, barbed wire, beer bottle caps, broken glass. She never once thought of this as cleaning up other people's messes, something she resented doing at home. She took these things back to her studio to see what she could make of them. She rolled cookie dough, cut out a new race of grotesque gingerbread people with broken glass eyes and beer-bottle-cap buttons. She cut out crosses and crucified them with broken nails and barbed wire. She disdained making mugs, bowls, plates. She wanted the clay to tell her something she didn't already know.

She took these things to city craft shops, but no one wanted to buy them. Now that she had deliberately made herself poor, she wanted to make some money. She didn't have a romantic view of being poor. She'd grown up in a coal mining town where poverty was as pervasive as soot. Her bank manager father had drilled into her what a privilege it was to be middle class. This made a hedonistic life impossible for Alice.

It prevented her from enjoying a family trip to California. The freeways rumbling with four-wheeled charioteers, swimming pools surrounded by tanned gods and goddesses, gardens of Lost Eden decaying with overripe fruit, all of it offended her sensibilities, her sense of deprivation. She expected the California earth to quake, rumble, to split open and swallow the station wagon into an abyss where gold miners, cowboys, movie stars writhed in fiery blackness. Alice couldn't wait to get back to Canada so she could put on sackcloth and ashes.

When she got home, she began to come apart, seamlessly. The unravelling didn't run in lines; instead, sores opened in unexpected places, holes with scabs picked off. She jumped when the phone rang. She forgot appointments. Her mind trailed off in the middle of sentences. She put the laundry in the garbage, the iron in the refrigerator. When she was in city traffic looking for a GE warehouse, tracking down a thirty-five-cent hinge for the dishwasher door, she got lost and ended up driving around crescents and deadends. She drifted through one animated intersection to another in the same way she had been conveyor-belted through Disneyland, before ramming into the rear of a new Firebird. The driver got out and called her a dumb broad, though it was her car, not his, that was bashed in.

After Alice had been in the Holy Rollers a month, she decided being two people suited her. Every morning after Gib and the kids went out the door, she slipped out of her velveteen housecoat — a Christmas present from Gib — got into old clothes and drove to her studio, where she exulted in sinking her hands into clay. The clay got under her fingernails, into the cracks of her skin, wiped onto her hair. She didn't bother washing it off to eat whatever food she had cached for lunch; usually it was crackers and sardines lifted out of oil with a dirty knife. She kept her studio as unadorned as a nun's cell, no pictures on the walls, no curtains, no rug on the floor. She thought the tools, the bottles, buckets and clay compositions spread helter-skelter across the room showed the birth of her true self which, for years, she had kept hidden inside a closet, a ghost too insubstantial to be X-rayed.

After she had been in the co-operative a month, Alice was voted in as a regular member. This was done at the monthly meeting, where the Holy Rollers sat on wooden chairs arranged in a circle on the paint-splattered floor. At this meeting, Alice got a look at the other members, most of whom she'd never seen before. They were art students who worked here on weekends and nights when Alice was someone else. She expected them to appear in old clothes, scruffy and unbarbered. She wasn't disappointed. Although Alice didn't have a romantic view of being poor, she certainly did when it came to being an artist. She thought being an artist required poverty, simplicity and, if necessary, sacrifice. She was impressed with sad eyes, El Greco beards, the lean and hungry look.

Most of the meeting was spent discussing money or lack of it. Like Alice, these artists couldn't sell their work; nobody wanted to buy it. This was because the establishment's taste was pedestrian and middle class. The Holy Rollers thought of themselves as refugees from the middle class. The newest refugee, Alice, cringed when she heard the words *middle class*. She thought her middle classness stood out all over her in bumps and warts. She hadn't sacrificed, she hadn't suffered. She agreed when the Holy Rollers branded the middle class as being too unquestioning, too self-satisfied, too smug, as drowning in its own mediocrity, distracted by affluence. What was needed, they said, was to simplify existence, pare it down to basic values, cut out the crap.

Listening to all this convinced Alice she was in the right place. She liked the democratic way the Holy Rollers was set up; it appealed to her penchant for fairness, the idea of being mutually responsible for each other, yet with enough privacy to do your own thing, the disregard for red tape and formality. The Holy Rollers shunned words like rules, parliamentary procedure, slate of officers. There was no way, however, of avoiding a treasurer; the rent had to be paid.

Lorne, the brown-bearded, hairy-chested sculptor, was treasurer. Before his reincarnation as an artist, he had been a public relations consultant with a mortgage, a wife and three kids; now he lived in a van with a young batik artist. Reading out of an ink-stained scribbler, he reported that the Holy Rollers owed the city three hundred dollars, which was a month's rent, a utility bill for $97.23 and a phone bill for $62.67. He suggested the co-operative mount an exhibit to raise money. If the Holy Rollers got on the media bandwagon to get the public in, he was sure it would be worth the effort. They would need a catchy name for the show; he suggested the Holy Roller Empire.

Lil was the only member of the co-operative whom Alice had come to know. This was probably because they were roughly the same age, which was forty-three, and they both worked in the daytime. Lil had the studio upstairs next to the bathroom. Sometimes when Alice was up there and Lil was taking a tea break, she'd invite Alice in for a cup of rosehip or camomile tea. Lil had about eight kinds of tea. It was her one luxury, she said. Lil eked out an existence heating tomato soup on a hot plate, eating Cheez Whiz sandwiches, spreading her Canada Council grant as far as it would go. She slept on a sofa in her studio. Her studio had a comfortable, cluttered feel about it. There were plants and light and Lil's paintings, which Alice liked. Her paintings were mural-sized da Vinci landscapes over which floated iridescent bubbles, each containing its own surrealistic world. Though she had a fine arts degree, Lil decided against teaching or getting married or having kids because she'd rather be hungry and free to paint. She exuded a calmness that Alice thought came from being alone. Lil was so skinny her hip bones were visible through her blue jeans. She had a narrow Cubist face and thin hair. Alice had the urge to ask Lil over for a home-cooked meal, chicken and dumplings, apple pie, but she suppressed the urge. She saw herself as two photographs, two black-and-white images, one in each hand. She wanted to keep it that way.

After Lil donated her work to the exhibit, the others donated theirs: batiks, prints, silkscreening, photographs, drawings, paintings, sculpture, pottery. A work weekend was organized to set up a gallery. While Gib and the kids went skiing, Alice and the other members hammered together flats and painted them white. The flats were arranged as a rectangular room in the open area where the washing machines had been. Artwork was hung on these walls. Plywood boxes, painted white, were set up for pottery and sculpture. After all the work was done, the Holy Rollers went out for beer. When Barry, a long-haired photographer who was sitting beside her in the bar, asked Alice if she was married — she had taken off her wedding ring when she was painting flats — she answered, sort of. This answer made Barry friendlier. He put his arm around her and gave her a squeeze. Alice was disgusted with herself; she loved her husband even if she was leading a double life.

Before the exhibit opened, Lorne called in reporters for photographs and interviews. He was on radio, television. Alice watched him being interviewed one night after the late news. His brown locks were curled into a Byronic cap, his chest gleamed with medallions, his gold fillings reflected the spotlights. He knew about camera angles, image-making. He hadn't been a public relations consultant for nothing. He talked about how a new, fast-growing, materialistic city needed grassroots artwork, how artists served the community by interpreting it; he emphasized the democratic nature of the co-operative, how any serious artist could become a member.

Members took turns tending the Holy Roller Empire. The night Alice's turn came round, it was thirty-five below. She didn't expect anyone would come but, with the media hoopla, Lorne said the door should be kept open until nine. About eight o'clock, two women came in, stamping snow off their sealskin boots. Alice was in her winter work uniform: hiking boots, jeans, fisherman's sweater, huddled over a space heater.

The women wore fur coats and hats. Ignoring Alice, they plunged headlong into the exhibit, giggling, bobbing their heads with the giddy wantonness of housewives who have been let out for an evening's fun and were determined to make the most of it. Alice looked at them. Suburban matrons, she thought, *middle class*, and picked up an art magazine.

But then she heard one of the women say something about gingerbread men, and she paid attention.

"Look at that, would you!" the woman said, indignant. "My daughter can do better than that!"

"Come on, Bea," the other woman said, "you know very well there's a hidden meaning in these things. You're just too dumb to get it."

Alice edged closer to the heater. Probably the woman's taste ran to velvet paintings.

The one named Bea arrived at Lil's painting, which had the place of honour at one end of the room. She looked at the painting. "You know, this thing could be hung upside down and you wouldn't know the difference," she said.

"If *I* had *that* in my living room," the other one said, "I'd hang it facing the wall."

"It wasn't meant to be hung in your living room," Alice said loudly. It was true these women had a right to dislike whatever they wanted, but she had the right to defend what she liked.

The fur coats jerked but didn't turn around. The women kept looking, passing remarks but carefully now.

Alice wondered why they had bothered coming in. To get warm was the answer. Probably they had been to a movie and were halfway to the parking lot. She wished they'd hurry up and go.

The one named Bea came over to Alice. "Is it true you have studios to rent?" she said.

Alice took the woman's interest as curiosity, nothing more. She'd no doubt seen Lorne on television.

"Yes," she said.

"How do I go about renting a studio?" Bea said. "Do I just walk in here with my easel or what?"

"You pay your rent and move in," Alice said. Carefully. She didn't think this woman could be serious. But the woman couldn't be denied information, could she? After all, a co-operative is supposed to be democratic.

"Is that what you did?" Bea said.

Alice nodded. It was clear this woman thought of her as an ally. Even in old clothes, she must look like a housewife. What was it that gave her away? Plucked eyebrows? Shiny hair? "The first month you're on probation. You're not a member until you're voted in," she said ominously.

"Oh, that won't bother me," Bea said breezily and smiled. She had a broad mouth, widely-spaced teeth, a face as open and flat as a prairie field. "I'll pop by first thing in the morning. Who do I see about the rent?"

"Lil Thorson. She's got the studio upstairs by the bathroom. She's always here. Sometimes I'm not," Alice said. She didn't want anything to do with this woman. And because she lived here, Lil had become the building's unofficial custodian. "You may not like it here at all," Alice warned her.

"This place isn't exclusive or anything like that, is it? I wouldn't want to get mixed up with anything exclusive," Bea said.

"It's anything but exclusive," Alice said. She really believed it.

"Good. Then I'll join. Strike while the iron's hot, I always say."

In the morning Alice heard footsteps thumping upstairs, furniture being dragged across the floor. Bea was moving in. Alice stayed in the basement as long as she could. Finally she had to go to the bathroom. She got up there all right but, as she was coming back along the hall, Bea nabbed her. She had rented the studio next to Lil's and wanted to show it off. She stood in the doorway of her studio, smock over her slacks, waiting for Alice to pass. She said, "Come on in."

Alice stuck her head in the door; it was as far as she wanted to go.

"How do you like it?" Bea said.

There was a shag rug on the floor, chintz curtains in the window, a chrome kitchen set with a pot of plastic ivy on it and a television screen splotched with domestic despair.

"My husband says it's just like home," Bea said proudly.

Alice took a quick look at the easel. Which was a mistake. Bea had taped a calendar picture of a rose to the board so she could paint it.

"Roses are my speciality," she said. "I think I must have done at least a hundred."

"You must know a rose off by heart," Alice said.

"Oh no," Bea said, "each rose is unique. You'd be surprised how they vary. They come in all shapes, all different stages of budding. Some with dew on them, some without. Then of course I have to change them colourwise to suit the room, depending on the commission."

"Commissions?" Alice said. "You have commissions?" Even Lil didn't have commissions.

"I've got five due next month. That's why I needed a studio in a hurry."

Alice fled downstairs and rolled out more clay. After talking to Bea, she was more determined than ever not to look for beauty in the conventional bowls and vases. She wanted to find a new kind of symmetry. She began making strange creatures, half-man, half-beast, people with seven legs, bulbous eyes, forked tongues.

For the rest of the week she succeeded in dodging Bea. This was possible because Bea kept the television turned up so loud she didn't hear Alice slip by her on her way to the bathroom. Alice noticed Lil had taken to keeping her door closed. Once she heard Lil banging on the wall and a voice so shrill Alice had trouble believing it was Lil's: "TURN OFF THE BLOODY TV!"

The second week, when Alice was going along the hall, a white poodle with a rhinestone collar and pink eyes rushed out of Bea's studio and yipped at her.

"Come here, Mitzi," Bea said.

A budgie will be next, Alice thought, a budgie in a glass cage. Or a goldfish with black tiddlywink eyes. She eased the dog away with her foot, gingerly.

"She won't bite," Bea assured her.

"I think you'd better keep your door closed," Alice told her. "Better still, keep the dog home."

"Can't," Bea said cheerfully, "she wets the rug if I do."

"Leave her in the car."

"Too cold. She'd freeze to death," Bea said. "She's not hurting anyone, is she?"

Alice had to admit the dog wasn't any trouble.

"Mitzi's my sister's dog," Bea explained. "That's why I can't leave her alone. She's upset because my sister's in the hospital. Breast cancer."

After Bea had been in the co-operative for three weeks, Lil came down to see Alice. She tapped on the KEEP OUT sign and asked if she could come in. Alice cleared a chair for her, but Lil wouldn't sit down. She stood there shifting from one foot to another, smoking a cigarette, drinking wine. She handed the bottle to Alice.

Alice poured some into a mug and handed the bottle back to Lil. Lil took a swig and sighed. "That woman is destroying my work habits," she said.

"The dog or the television?"

"Both. And her unnerving habit of interrupting me."

"Tell her to stop," Alice said. "Remind her about members' rights."

"I already have, but she can't seem to remember from one day to the next. She's in my studio every day with some excuse. She's run out of titanium white, where do we keep our toilet paper, did somebody turn down the thermostat, would I like a cup of instant. On and on."

"What about getting her studio switched?" Alice knew there was no question of Lil switching. After all, she was a founding member of the Holy Rollers.

Lil sighed again. "She's got the last one. Wouldn't you know, for months we have all these empty studios to rent, then, when we've one more to go, someone like her turns up?"

"Maybe when she finishes these commissions, she'll leave on her own," Alice said.

"I doubt it," Lil said. "I'll tell you one thing. If she's still here at the end of the month, I'm having her voted out."

The next afternoon Alice went outside into twenty-five-below weather and found her car had a flat tire. It was two-thirty and she had to take her son to a three o'clock orthodontic appointment she'd waited six weeks for. She got the rear end of the car jacked up without difficulty. It was the bolts she had trouble with. They'd been screwed on with an impact wrench and wouldn't come off. Alice had to go inside three times to warm her hands. At three o'clock, when she was making her fourth attempt, Bea came out to get into her car and came over to help.

"Looks like the threads on your wrench are worn," she said. She went over to her car and came back with her wrench. She got two bolts off with it but the rest wouldn't budge.

While they were struggling with these last bolts, Lorne came out of the laundry and got into his van. He had to pass them to do this, but he didn't offer to help.

After he had driven away, Bea looked at Alice and said, "Are they all like that?"

They never did get the remaining bolts off and Bea drove Alice home. Alice made a new appointment.

A week later, at the monthly meeting, Alice was astonished to see Bea turn up in a lilac pantsuit, chartreuse scarf and orange finger-nails that matched her hair. Bea had been here a month, long enough to learn something about protecting herself.

The meeting started with Lorne reporting that so far the exhibit had only made $167, which barely paid for the lumber and paint. The arctic weather had no doubt affected sales; he recommended leaving the exhibit open for another month.

"It isn't the weather," Bea said. Though she hadn't been voted in as a member, it didn't prevent her from speaking up. "Most of the stuff in the exhibit is too far-out. Nobody wants to put that kind of thing in their houses."

"Spoken like a true Sunday painter," Lil said.

Bea got the message and shut up.

The members voted to keep the exhibit open another month.

Lorne asked the new members to leave the room; it was time for them to be voted on. Two art students and Bea filed out. There was no discussion about the students; they got in without question. But when Bea's name came up, Lil had a lot to say. "I don't think she belongs here," she said. She recited a list of complaints, ending up with, "The kindest thing we can do is ask her to leave." As if Bea were a stray dog that had to be put away.

Alice abstained from the vote.

When Lorne told her that the members felt she'd be happier working elsewhere, Bea put on her fur coat and picked up her handbag. Matter-of-factly, as if she'd expected it. But she couldn't have expected it, Alice thought, otherwise she wouldn't have turned up at the meeting.

"I was thinking of leaving anyway," Bea said. "The reason I came here in the first place was that my nephews took over the bedroom I painted in and, with these commissions hanging over my head, I needed a place to finish them up."

Why did Bea add this? Did she think anyone would care where she painted? Or was she one of these people who needed to make explanations?

When Bea got to the doorway, she said, "Oh, by the way, I got all five commissions done while I was here. That's a thousand dollars!"

"I'll look for your work in the Westview Mall," someone sniped after her. Not Lil.

All of which made Alice regret having abstained. Having impaled herself on a treetop, arms outstretched, a photograph in each hand. She was weary of maintaining this position and ashamed of her naïveté. In the rarefied atmosphere of her studio with the KEEP OUT sign on the door, she had actually thought she could stay on the treetop.

Once she got her feet on the ground, Alice wasn't long in finding something that suited her better.

Not long after she left the Holy Rollers, she was back in her Volkswagen driving out of the city, taking the old road to the mountains. She passed a FOR SALE sign on a fence post. Ordinarily she wouldn't have stopped; real estate didn't interest her. But she saw the snowy field had a small church on it. She got out of the car, walked across the field making clean footprints in the snow. The church was white clapboard with a pioneer squareness about it. Except for the spire and a red and yellow stained-glass window over the door, it might have been a school.

Alice looked in the windows at the hard, wooden pews, the raised platform in the front, the coat rack at the back. She walked around the outside of the church, the sun glancing off the snow, the cold air cutting her breath, the sky blue to the mountains. There wasn't a tree or even a shrub in the field. This flatness wasn't a landscape she was drawn to, but she had to start somewhere.

She thought about buying this church. She'd have to borrow the money, find a paying job for a couple of years, but it could be done. She looked in the window again. The platform was big enough for a studio area. She could build shelves against the railing, replace the pulpit with her wheel. There was still enough space left over for living quarters. In the spring, when the frost was out of the ground, she could dig a hole, put in coals, and wrap grass, roots, prairie crocuses, whatever she could find around her pottery, and fire it primevally.

Gib and the kids could come out on weekends for picnics, hiking, fishing. She looked at the frozen landscape hopefully, knowing that, underneath this ice and snow, there had to be water someplace.

From a High Thin Wire

All the way home, I kept telling people: the ticket agent, the stewardess, the woman who sat beside me on the plane; to anyone who would listen, I said: "My mother is dead." I wanted to hear their voices soften sympathetically, to see their eyes cloud over, mirroring my own, hidden behind dark glasses.

My sister got home two days before me. I find it ironic that she, who had never been as close to my mother as I, should arrive first, that she should be the one to make the decisions, the arrangements. I resent this; even Death, I'm surprised to discover, does not exterminate Pandora's insects, and they still fly about, aiming poisoned needles right on target.

There is an explanation for my delay. I was on holidays when the accident happened, camping in the mountains. A carrier pigeon would have been faster than the Mounties trying to find me. And I would have preferred a messenger from the air containing three words, *she is dead*, in its ankle band. I would have found the message more appropriate seeing it in print, winged over fields, lakes, prairies and mountains. And I would have believed it.

Instead, I didn't believe it. There was this man swaying in front of me, bubbling words into the underwater air between us, mouthing strange, incredible words about my mother being killed in an accident. I had to bang my head against the plank table to knock sense into this bizarre undersea creature, stop him from bubbling nonsense, drown him, make him go away.

But the man took me by the hand and led me to the car. He put me in the front seat and the children in the back. Then we drove away. After a while, I turned around and looked at the children's faces, which were soft, crumpled. They kept their eyes averted, gazing hard out the window; they couldn't look at my face because I was their mother. I knew then that the man beside me must be my husband, and he was taking me to catch a plane.

Jane is at the airport to meet me. With her usual foresight, she rented a U-Drive as soon as she arrived from Montreal. I see her standing at the end of the waiting crowd, separate from the rest. Is she really separate from them, I wonder, or is it that I think of her as being separate, smarter, superior? She too is wearing dark glasses, and I notice her usually tailored hair is untidy like mine.

There is a wait for my bag, and then we are on the road driving home. Both of us married with children living far away, and we call this town home. As children, "home" was carried with us from place to place. It was always a town. For a while, it was this town we are driving into, with its lazy winding river dreaming memories of Saturday swims, its long Main Street lined with elms arching overhead, shading the pavement from the hot sun. It's summer, and as we near the cenotaph which marks the centre of town, we notice the tourist cars with their foreign licence plates, mostly American and Upper Canadian, one each from Alberta and BC. They have come to buy ice cream, because this town advertises itself as the Dairy Centre of the Maritimes, and to shop for local crafts. It has taken others, Americans among them, to exalt these rural skills, to shape the local clays into the natural grace of hearth-bound pottery, to weave the sheep rancher's wool into cushion covers and placemats, to polish stones casually found on Sunday picnics into symbolic jewellery — oracle pendants and birthstone rings.

Across from the cenotaph is Millar's Funeral Home. "Home" again. I have difficulty thinking of this square grey building, newly painted, as home. All those afternoons I walked past it on the way home from school and I never noticed Millar's Funeral Home, though it was there in a row with Prescott's Insurance and the feed store, none of them part of my world then. Back then, I didn't know anyone who was in Millar's. Now I do. Jane has told me. I'm disappointed to hear this because I know my mother wanted to be cremated. Because it was an accident, there was the delay of an investigation. Even if I had arrived earlier, cremation might not have been possible because the body would have had to be sent by train to the city crematorium, which would have taken more time. I don't mention my mother's preference to Jane. Only I know of my mother's wish to be cremated. I'm proud of being the only one to know this, of being my mother's confidante.

For a long time, my mother couldn't talk to Jane. But when Jane was a little girl and I a baby too young to talk, Jane used to babble on, sharing secrets, telling my mother everything that had happened in school. She used to show her stories she had printed, pictures she had drawn. My mother used to tape them to the wall behind the stove, where, I noticed when mine were put there, they got grease splattered on them, and eventually, after the steam loosened the tape, they fell to the floor and were forgotten in the dust behind the stove. Jane started tacking her stories and pictures in a neat square on the wall beside the bed; later, she got a bulletin board.

"Do you want to see her before we go to the house?" Jane says.

"Have you seen her yet?"

"No," Jane says and no more. Since I've just arrived, I can make the decision. Is she as reluctant as I am? She's driving so efficiently it is hard to tell. I don't expect Jane to crack open. I never forget she is three and a half years older than me. I still think of her as bigger and stronger, though we are the same size.

Though the funeral parlour director has made some effort to lighten the room with high ceilings, classical mouldings and lighting fixtures disguised as candelabras, the air in front of me wavers darkly. I am inside an underwater grotto at the end of which is a rock shelf. On the shelf is an elongated shape. It is a long walk to the end of the room. I stare down at her, gift-boxed in white satin with gold trim; even the inside cover of the casket is lined with elaborate foldings of white satin and pink rosettes. She's wearing a blue-grey dress buttoned down the front, an ugly dress she never wore, taken from the back of her closet. Why isn't she wearing a sweater and slacks? Why must it be a dress? Her hands are folded in an unfamiliar gesture, her left hand with its silver wedding band carefully placed on top. The waxy mouth is too wide, the face too long, the cheeks heavily rouged. The wavy hair, which neither Jane nor I inherited, is the only part of her that's right. I am looking at a corpse, not a person. This corpse, pieced together and touched up, isn't my mother.

When we get to the house, Jane parks the car while I wait on the doorstep with my bag until she unlocks the front door. Inside it is cool and dark, kept that way by the elm trees towering overhead. We step into the living room, and the familiarity of its furniture comes back to me. It's not the furniture itself but its juxtaposition that I'm seeing, the arrangement of these objects: the lantern lamp, the colonial rocker, the marble-topped table. This was the same furniture moved from house to apartment, from apartment to farmhouse, from farmhouse to bungalow, from bungalow to duplex, from duplex to apartment and, finally, to this house. It was always after we got the furniture "arranged," each piece set in its immutable place, that we began to feel at home.

Jane has scorned this careless eclecticism. She has done it right, employing an interior designer to decorate her Westmount home. Once, when Jane and I were passing through the furniture section of a large department store on one of my visits to her, she stopped beside a hybrid chair, all stripes and curlicues, amused by its ugliness.

"That reminds me of Mother," she said.

My mother didn't care about furniture. It didn't matter to her, she said. But I remember long ago, in our first house, we had a Persian rug, heavy rose-coloured drapes and matching plush furniture. Here in this room, gilt-framed watercolour flowers hang on the wall, relics from those prosperous days.

I go into the bedroom and unpack my bag. Jane makes tea. While we drink it, we nibble at a plateful of squares the neighbours have sent in. Though my mother was careful with neighbours, they have responded with unexpected kindness, bringing in plates of muffins, biscuits and sweets. Jane says there are three casseroles in the fridge. She takes out her list from beneath the napkin holder and begins ticking off the items. My sister organizes herself with lists, making monthly lists and, from them, weekly lists. I see her in front of me now, a square-shouldered, well-proportioned woman, wearing a patchwork garment of lists. There is necessity in this attire; it's by making lists that Jane runs an efficient home: meals on time, cupboards well stocked, socks mended.

For a while she tried to run my mother, a disorganized, forgetful housekeeper who often overlooked buying Jane's Kotex with the groceries, as Jane had instructed her to do. Jane wouldn't buy it herself; she was fifteen and preoccupied with denying her womanhood, disguising her full breasts with baggy blouses and loose dresses, refusing to wear a sweater.

My mother was tired; she had no intention of going back to the store, it was high time Jane bought her own Kotex. Both of them looked at me — gangling, awkward, still indifferent to female body functions. I could do it easily. I was quick to recognize my role as intermediary. I wanted one of Jane's unworn sweaters that hung, washed and pressed, each on its own hanger in her closet. Jane didn't want to lend me one because, she said, it would end up under my bed. I drove a hard bargain.

So casually did I treat this errand that I didn't go straight home but left the Kotex in my bicycle carrier while I spent the afternoon at a friend's. When I got home, Jane snatched the Kotex out of my hands and refused to lend me a sweater. I wrenched the box back, raking her arm with my fingernails when she wouldn't give it up. She pulled my hair until I went down on my knees.

"I ordered my flowers. Red roses," Jane is saying now. "They'll be delivered later on today. I left yours for you to order."

"I'm not ordering any."

"You of all people should know how much she loved flowers," she reproaches me.

"Of course, but not hothouse flowers. Outside flowers. Wildflowers."

Jane says nothing. She's grown used to rustic extravagances; one of her daughters is a flower child who wears embroidered jeans, peasant blouses, daisies in her hair.

"I'll put them in her favourite black bowl. You know, the one with the rounded sides."

Jane doesn't know.

"You'll have to take them over today," she says doubtfully, "because tonight we have to receive visitors."

"Do we have to do that? She knew so few people here."

"That's what I said, but the funeral director said you had to let people pay their respects. Let the people of the town show they care."

The people of the town. How many towns had my mother lived in? Not cities but small towns where, as they say, you really get to know people. My mother seldom got to know people, though she once told me that, when she was younger, she knew a lot of people. When she was a little girl, she used to perform in front of company, dancing and singing. My grandmother, she said, called her a song sparrow. But when she was nine, she stopped singing. That was the year my grandmother died and my mother was sent to board with a miserly witch, fairy-tale mean, who put her to work scrubbing floors and took her clothing allowance so that she went to school with hand-me-downs on her back and holes in her shoes. Until she ran away to another woman, who was kinder and mercifully liked to sew dresses for a little girl.

There are a few spiky delphiniums and dried-out marigolds in the garden; she hadn't been well since spring and had let the garden go. But walking up the street over the hill past the modern bungalows built on the edge of town, I come upon a field full of buttercups. I pick them carefully. From here, I can see the town below; the long line of guardian elms, one church spire sticking up, the willows following the river.

When I finish arranging the buttercups in the black bowl, Jane stops answering the sympathy cards that came in today's mail and brings out her list, timing her efforts with mine.

"Do you feel up to sorting out her clothes?" she says.

"If you are."

My mother saved everything: lace hankies in flat purses, sheer nighties, seashell earrings, pastel gloves, all unworn. We empty the drawers onto the bed and begin to sort. Underneath the lingerie, we find a sewing card that I had given her one Mother's Day. It's a girl in a sunbonnet watering flowers, and on the back is printed in wobbly letters: *To Mother, Love Gwen.* We find our elementary school report cards. Comparing them, we find that we weren't as smart or as well-behaved in school as she had led us to believe. Whenever I asked her about ourselves when we were younger, she would say impartially, Both you girls were good, I was lucky you were so good.

Jane and I know better. That is why we are desperate now not to own her belongings, neither of us wanting to gain anything from the void, from the wavering emptiness beneath our feet. In any case, little of it fits us. Our mother was smaller and more delicately boned than we. We are tall women, Jane and I, strong pioneer Scots. We bag most of her clothes for the church, and I marvel how, in the end, the exotic bathrobe we had once coveted could be dispatched to a stranger with such eagerness.

When we are done, Jane takes a blue velvet box from her purse and hands it to me. "I asked Mr. Millar to take it off. I think she would have wanted you to have it."

It's my mother's silver engagement ring. I have never liked diamonds, but I take the ring. I will give it to my daughter some day and tell her it was her grandmother's. Now that our family has dwindled down to Jane and me, I've become concerned about family heirlooms.

Then she says, "Do you know she nearly left him once?"

This comes as a surprise, that Jane should know something about my mother that I don't.

"About eight years ago, she phoned and said he wanted to move again. She couldn't take another move, another business. Starting all over. She wanted to stay here. Would it be all right if she visited us for a month until she decided what to do?"

Was it because I lived farther away that she didn't ask to stay with me?

"She only stayed a week because that was when he had his first heart attack. She felt guilty of course, not being there when he had it, even though it was a mild one. It's a terrible thing to say, but I think in a way she was relieved by that first attack because it meant they could stay where they were. I mean, it settled things once and for all. She would never have admitted that, of course."

After supper, Jane and I go to Millar's Funeral Home, Jane carrying her notebook, me my bowl of buttercups. The flowers, she reminds me, will have been delivered by now, and we will need to list those to whom we must write thank-you notes.

I place the bowl on the table beside the guest book, which is open, ready for signatures.

"It should be nearer the casket," Jane points out, "where the family flowers are supposed to be."

"No," I say stubbornly. "I'd rather have it here by itself."

Jane goes over to check her flowers, a large spray of red roses, three dozen of them fanned out at the foot of the casket.

I expect her to be pleased by their traditional opulence. They are Jane's style, they would easily fit into her French Provincial living room, but she's far from pleased. She reaches out and grabs

From a High Thin Wire

the strip of red ribbon embossed in gold. From Your Loving Daughter, it says in script. It won't come away easily, and she has to yank hard before the ribbon will come off the wire stalk.

"Imagine!" she says fiercely, stuffing the ribbon into her purse. "Putting that kind of thing on my flowers. Don't they know any better?"

At first I think she's offended by the sentimentality of the inscription, but then she says, "It wasn't like that at all."

The people of the town come in then, a slow tide of warm hands, a quicksand of words: a terrible accident, so sudden, such a lovely person she was, she was so proud of you girls.

Jane and I are surprised that so many people are showing up to pay their respects. In cities, accidents such as this are commonplace — you see the paragraph allotted to each one on the first page of the second section of the newspaper; it almost seems a luxury to mourn the death of one person when hundreds, thousands are killed in plane crashes, tornadoes, earthquakes. But in small towns, all it takes is the death of a single person to spell out the proximity of death. These people in front of me, shaking hands, have come to register this fact. Though they only saw our mother on the street and in the stores, they recognized her vulnerability, her particular loneliness. She sang two notes from a high thin wire, and they have come to say they heard them.

By ten o'clock, the visitors have gone, and Jane and I are preparing to leave.

We are at the doorway when two women come at us from across the hall, where they have been viewing a man, his emaciated frame laden with medals, a veteran from the war whose only floral tribute is a Remembrance Day wreath of plastic leaves and poppies.

I don't know either of these women, though one looks vaguely familiar. She's wearing rhinestone earrings and a necklace and a white hat with a veil. She has a harelip, probably that is why I remember her. I've seen her on the street during one of my visits home. The other woman I've never seen before. She too is hatted and gloved. Her face is heavily made up, masked in rouge, brownish pancake base, slash of lipstick above her sagging chin. I shake hands and ask them to sign the guest book. The woman with the harelip declines but stands eyeing my buttercups critically while the other writes down her name, Cora Webster, then where she's from.

She isn't from this town but from another one up the valley.

Jane sits in the chair beside the door, takes out her list, waiting for them to go. The two women walk slowly, ritualistically toward the end of the room. They hardly glance at the casket but begin with the flowers. The one from out of town, Cora, cannot see the cards, either because the room is too dimly lit or because she's too vain to wear her glasses. But the woman with the harelip isn't vain. She takes out her glasses and, stooping over, reads off the cards. She does this methodically, starting at one end, Cora following alongside, moving past a pedestal bearing a flower basket, then wire stands of sprays designed two-dimensionally so they can be laid on the grave afterwards.

At last, they came to the corpse.

"Do you know her?" Cora asks in a loud whisper.

"Never laid eyes on her," the woman with the harelip answers.

"What's her name again?" Cora whispers back.

"Ruth. Ruth Somebody. I forget." Then, not bothering to keep her voice down, the woman goes on, "They fixed her up real good, didn't they? They do a *lovely* job in here. She was a *real mess* they said. When the truck hit her, it was *so loud* you could hear the noise clear up to the corner."

Both of them are bending over the casket taking in the details: the nylons with a run, the wedding band, plain, simple, the dress conservative enough — not too new yet without signs of wear.

"Get out!" I say from the doorway. I haven't moved from this spot, though my eyes have been following them. If I'd moved closer, I might not have been able to do it but, as it is, I am going through with it, plunging on. "How dare you come in here! You didn't even know her!" I'm shouting now. "Get out!"

They say nothing, though their eyes blink and their mouths hang open. They tilt their chins up, heads back, trying not to look like the vultures they are. And I stand at the door bullying them, making them flap past me, wings clipped, claws hooked onto their purses.

There's a suggestion of a smile on Jane's face, but she knows better than to let it show. Instead she says, drily snapping her purse shut, "You always did have a temper."

"So did you," I flare back at her. Then I see the light go out of her face and I remember the ribbon in her purse. I shouldn't have reminded her. I got even with her a long time ago. When Jane wouldn't let go of my hair and I wouldn't let go of the Kotex box until she lent me a sweater, I called for my mother. When she came to my defence, Jane let go of me and grabbed my mother, turned her over her knee and spanked her. That evening our father gave Jane the spanking of her life. And I was allowed to keep her best sweater.

As we leave Millar's Funeral Home, I am feeling strangely, perversely reckless.

"Let's go for a walk," I say. "Let's go to the creamery."

The creamery was where she was killed, in front of it on Main Street, not on some unpaved back street hidden away in trees but in full view on Main Street.

We step onto the sidewalk. It is grey dark with a silky coolness coming up from the river spreading over the hot pavement. There might be a fog tonight, I think, already it might be creeping in from the sea forty miles away, easing its way up the valley, sliding silently through the night so that, in the morning, a cool mist will envelop the town, relieving the heat built up these past few weeks.

The moon is up now, round and bright. It rinses the pavement in front of the creamery in pale light. The air over the pavement shimmers like water, a pulsating mirage.

"This is where it happened." Jane points to the crosswalk.

"It's an open stretch. Why didn't the driver see her?"

"He did. He tooted the horn, but she didn't stop. She was hooked onto the truck mirror and thrown back under the wheels."

Jane is speaking reportorially now; it's her duty to spare me nothing. "Both her legs, all her ribs were broken, her skull bashed in." Then she adds, "She was carrying an ice cream cone."

She adds this as if it's irrelevant, but it isn't.

Little old lady, silver-haired, frail, carrying an ice cream cone across the road, watching it melt in the heat. Gravel truck bursting down black pavement, tearing the last page of a wishful story into fluttering pieces. It's the same incongruity I see between her and us: she, a small bird, bones broken, a sparrow lying on the pavement, and Jane and I, our shadows enlarged by the streetlight into broad, gullish shapes.

"She did a good job," I say. Then, when Jane doesn't respond, I add, "Or don't you think so?"

Abruptly Jane swings away. She's not going to answer.

But, as she turns, I see that she is saying something after all. Her lips are opening, letting out words that rise singly like air bubbles floating slow motion through water. Except that, when her words reach the surface, they become rough-edged explosions.

"Of course I think so," she says. She reaches over then and shakes me crossly, her fingernails biting deep into my arm. "We learned to fly," she says. "Isn't that enough?"